WHISKERS

WHISKERS

Donald W. Kruse

ZACCHEUS ENTERTAINMENT
Minong, WI

Whiskers by Donald W. Kruse is published by:

ZACCHEUS ENTERTAINMENT

Zaccheus Entertainment
P.O. Box 23
Minong, WI 54859

ISBN: 978-0-9994571-4-6

1st Edition copyright 2009

2nd Edition copyright 2019

Cover Illustration by Craig Howarth

Manufactured in the United States of America

A special thank you from the author to Craig Howarth.

To Dean Koontz—

*a good man
with a kind heart
and one of my
favorite authors*

ACKNOWLEDGMENTS

I thank God for the gift of writing. And a very special thank you to Ms. Phyllis Diller who taught me, "Onward and Upward!" I love you, My Lady.

And with love to my wife, Marilyn, who is blazing a trail with me through life's precarious journey. For 47 years, we've lived, we've loved, and we've endured. And along the way, by our example, we have silenced the naysayers!

CHAPTER 1

"Now remember, Greg—you're in charge. Keep your eye on the twins, and don't fight with your sister."

Greg rolled his eyes. "I know, Mom. You already told me that. You've been telling me that for the entire trip up here."

Dad poked his head out from the rear of the station wagon, his brow lowered. "Grab the rest of these suitcases, Greg, and don't sass your mother."

Biting his lip, Greg glanced at Jenny, his 14-year-old sister, who was, as he suspected, smirking at him. She always smirked at him whenever Mom or Dad yelled at him or scolded him. She can't wait until I get in trouble, he thought, leaning his six-foot frame into the back of the wagon. He grasped the handles on two large, gray suitcases and lifted them effortlessly from the car. He set them in the sand next to the other luggage, then took a deep breath, trying to curb his anger. The fresh, pleasing aroma of northwestern Wisconsin jack pine filled his nostrils. Exhaling slowly, he felt his tension slipping away. "I'm sorry, Mom. I didn't mean to sass you. It's just that sometimes I get the feeling you don't trust me with Jenny or the twins." He looked deep into Mom's face, noting how young she still looked at 45.

Here I am, he thought, 17 years old and just graduated from high school, and my mother still doesn't have wrinkles or gray hair. I'll probably be gray before her—thanks to Jenny and the twins. "You know I wouldn't let anything happen to them, Mom."

Mom smiled her usual warm smile and started to speak, but Dad cut her off.

"Just the same, I don't want anymore bickering on this trip," Dad said gruffly. "You kids have done nothing but fight and argue in the car for the last eight hours, and I want it stopped." He set a large, blue and white cooler down on the cabin steps, then turned and looked at Greg, wiping his brow. "Understand?"

At six-foot-four, two hundred and fifty pounds, with the temper of a wolverine, Dad was definitely no one to sass.

Greg felt himself tighten against the stifling authority. "Yes, sir," he said, through his teeth. He glanced at Jenny, whose face was smeared into one giant smirk. A hundred million sisters in the world, he thought, and I get stuck with *her*—little miss brat of the universe. Daddy's little pet.

The twins, Timmy and Tommy, were running around the car, giggling and hollering, chasing Spook, the family dog. Spook was a hundred-pound German shepherd who, Greg thought, spent the greater time of its life trying to avoid the twins. Spook slipped in the sand just long enough for Tommy to latch on to the dog's tail. Then Timmy caught up with them and pounced on Spook, wrapping his arms around the dog's neck, hanging from it like a rag doll. Spook yelped and bucked like a wild horse, but Timmy held on with all the skill of a seasoned broncobuster. But it wasn't until Tommy yanked on the tail and twirled it like a piece of rope when Spook finally growled and showed his teeth.

Greg turned and looked at Dad, who was staring in shocked

disbelief at the ruckus. How long is he going to let *this* go on? he thought, watching Dad's face growing redder and redder.

"Timmy and Tommy! KNOCK IT OFF!" Dad yelled, veins popping from his forehead. "You wanna get bi—"

Too late. With a bloodcurdling growl, Spook wrestled free of Timmy's choke hold and nipped his arm. His big teeth still gnashing, Spook spun around and bit Tommy's hand before Tommy had a chance to let go of the dog's tail.

The twins screamed and ran to Mom, holding their wounds, their freckled faces streaming with tears.

"I told you to leave that dog alone!" Dad shouted. "Didn't I tell you boys he'd bite you sooner or later? Didn't I tell you?"

The twins buried their faces in Mom's waist, their crew-cut heads jerking with each sob.

Mom frowned at Dad. "Leave 'em alone, Sam," she said, wrapping her arms protectively around the twins. "I think they've learned their lesson."

Give me a *break!* Greg thought, rolling his eyes, pulling a box of groceries from the car. Spook could've bitten off both their hands and they'd still come back to tease him. Who was she kidding?

Mom stroked the twins' fuzzy heads. "Come on now, everybody. This is no way to start a vacation. My goodness, let's not let a little car ride spoil everything. Everybody's probably just a little tired and hungry and crabby from the long trip, but you'll all feel better after a nice meal and a good night's sleep. Okay, everybody? Now all you men pitch in and get the car unloaded, and me and Jenny will go in and get supper started." Mom marched up the front steps, opened the screen door, then stopped and turned around. "And remember, everybody, we're here to have *fun*. Okay?"

Jenny let a clump of her long, brown hair that she had been chewing on drop from her mouth. A strand of it still clung to her silvery braces. "What's for dinner, Mom?" she asked, following Mom inside.

What a slob, Greg thought, watching her pick the strand from her teeth. He was about to remark on it, then remembered Dad's stern warning about any further bickering. She'll probably have that stupid hair all over our dinner, he thought, following the women inside with the suitcases. She may have a slender figure and polished nails, but she's definitely a pig. On his way out, he held the door open for Timmy and Tommy, who were struggling to bring in a large cardboard box.

Tommy looked up at Greg, his brown eyes wide with excitement. "This is the box with the wemote contwol boats in it!" he sputtered, his tongue flicking in and out of the gap where his two front teeth used to be.

Timmy exploded with excitement, too, at the mere mention of the remote control boats. "Yeah! An-an-an-and you know what, Gweg? You-you-you wanna know what?"

Greg smiled, trying hard not to laugh. Cute little twerps, he thought, when they're not being bratty. "What, Timmy?"

"Ummmm ... my-my-my boat is fassss-tor than Tommy's."

"It is not!" Tommy shot back, insulted.

"Yeah, it is!"

"No, it's not!"

"Is too!"

"Is not!"

"Yeah, it is!"

"All right, all right, you guys," Greg said. "Tell you what ... after supper, we'll go down to the lake and race 'em. Then we'll *know* whose is the fastest. Okay?"

The twins' freckled faces lit up like Christmas trees. "Oh, boy!" they cried. "Mom, is sup-por done yet?"

Greg didn't want to show it, but he shared the twins' excitement over the remote control boats. Ever since he was a little kid, he had a fascination for remote control toys: boats, cars, and planes. Being able to control the toys, making them speed up, slow down, making figure 8's, or crashing them into things thrilled him. It was a thrill he had never outgrown. For as long as he could remember, his hobbies had always been centered around the fast and daring and potentially dangerous: scuba diving, karate, pistol target practice, dirt bike racing, and snowmobiling. Racing his remote control toys was actually the safest of his hobbies. What the heck, he thought, it's fun!

After a supper of hot dogs, macaroni and cheese, and tossed salad, Timmy and Tommy unpacked the remote control boats. There was a red one for Timmy, and a yellow one for Tommy. The boats were tiny replicas of actual speedboats, complete with miniature propellers, plastic windshields, and chrome railings. If the lake water was smooth with no waves, the boats could reach a top speed of five miles per hour.

I bet that seems pretty fast to a little kid, Greg thought, watching the twins insert the battery packs into the boats. "Come on, you guys. The last one down to the lake is a rotten egg."

Timmy and Tommy scooped up their boats and remote control boxes, then bolted through the screen door, letting it snap shut with a bang. Spook charged after them, banging his head against the screen. The door flew open, and he bounded out, his tail swishing frantically, his happy barking echoing throughout the surrounding woods.

Greg snatched his fishing rod from a corner rack and started for the door. "Might as well get in a little fishing on the first day of vacation."

Mom eyed him with the rod, and her face became clouded with worry. "Don't forget to keep an eye on them, Greg."

He started to sigh, then caught himself. "I will, Mom. I promise."

Dad came out of the bedroom, carrying a plaid, canvas suitcase. "Greg, before you go, take this out to the car."

Greg thought he was joking. He waited for Dad to smile, but the smile never came. Instead, Dad held the suitcase out to him, expecting Greg to take it without complaint. Puzzled, Greg stared at Dad as if the big guy were nuts. "We just got done unloading them all," he said cautiously.

"I know, but your mother and I have decided to leave tonight for that pest control convention in Pine Acres. There's gonna be over a thousand exterminators there, and we wanna make sure we get a good seat. Can you imagine that?—over a thousand exterminators. And a lot of them are fellow pest control business owners."

Big deal, Greg thought, trying not to show his disgust. How in the world can a grown man get excited about a pest control convention? Just a bunch of exterminators sitting around, talking about bugs and rodents. How stupid. And they're always telling *me* to grow up and act my age.

"Yeah, that's nice, Dad," he said, grabbing the suitcase with his free hand. "Hope you have fun."

"Yeah, and we gotta drive right past that nuclear power plant that was on the news not too long ago. After spending millions of dollars to build it, they closed it down after only a few years. They found out it was cheaper to burn coal, but you would've thought they would've known that *before* they built it and wasted all that money. And now they're stuck with tons of radioactive plutonium rods, with no place else to store them. What a fiasco." Dad disappeared briefly behind the bedroom curtain, then returned, holding a sealed five-gallon metal pail. "This stuff is heavy," he said, straining against the weight.

"What's that?" Greg asked.

"It's a pesticide called Chlordane. We use it to kill termites. It's mean stuff—very deadly. The government has banned its manufacture in this country, but we're allowed to use up whatever we have left in stock. The only problem is, I don't do any termite work anymore, so I thought I'd give this to someone at the convention. Out of a thousand exterminators, there ought to be *someone* there who can use it."

"Why don't you just dump it in the lake?" Greg asked nonchalantly.

Dad was already headed for the door, but stopped abruptly when he heard Greg's question. He set the heavy pail down next to the door and spun around, his face hard and stern. He marched up to Greg, looming over him. "What are you ... stupid?" he barked. Then he started counting his fingers. "Number one, it's illegal to dump pesticides in a lake or a river or a stream or in any body of water. Number two, this stuff is so strong, so deadly, it would kill everything in the lake—fish, turtles, frogs, ducks, loons, snakes, you name it. Number three, don't you ever *think* before you talk?"

Mom turned around from the kitchen sink where she and Jenny were washing the dinner dishes. "Take it easy, Sam."

Greg was startled by Dad's verbal assault. What the heck is *your* problem? he thought. Well, excuuuuuse me! But he didn't say a word. He just stood and stared, confused.

Dad stared back, as if he were just waiting for Greg— almost challenging him—to talk back.

But only Mom spoke. "Now remember, Greg, keep your eye on the twins, and don't fight with your sister. We'll be gone for four days, and we're leaving you in charge."

Impulsively, Greg pounded the butt of his fishing rod on the pine plank floor. "You already tol—" A severe look from Dad stopped him in mid-sentence. "Okay, Mom."

Dad raised his eyebrows and looked at Jenny. "Of course, if you kids want to, you can all come along with us to the convention. We'll be staying at a fancy hotel, with an indoor pool and a real nice restaurant."

Jenny whirled around from the sink, her hands dripping with soapy dishwater. "Oh, Dad, please! We're supposed to have *fun* on our vacation." She turned to Mom. "Mom, please don't make us go with. Please?"

Keeping her eyes glued on the dinner plate she was drying with a white terry towel, Mom shrugged. "It's up to you."

"Thanks, Mom," Jenny said, exhaling deeply, obviously relieved.

Dad lowered his brow, his face stern again. "Then make darn sure you behave yourself while we're gone, young lady. And don't fight with your brothers."

She insulted him, Greg thought, laughing to himself. Now *she's* in trouble. As he brushed past her, his fishing rod in one hand, the suitcase in the other, he gave her a full-scale smirk that said, "Ha, ha on you."

Jenny fired a hateful look at him, her eyes narrowed, her lips scrunched up in a knot.

How do *you* like it, brat? he thought. Feeling victorious, he strutted out the door, letting it bang shut. "Have a nice trip," he called over his shoulder. "And don't worry about a thing—we'll be fine."

"Just the same," Dad said, "if you have any problems, you've got your cell phone, and you can always go to Tucker Island. Mr. and Mrs. Tucker will be glad to help you, and it's only twenty minutes by boat."

"Okay, Dad."

"Oh," Mom said, "if you see Mrs. Tucker, tell her I said hello. And tell her I'll come over to visit as soon as we get back from our trip. I haven't seen Mrs. Tucker since last summer. I did send her a Christmas card last December, though. I hope she's all right—poor old soul. She hasn't been the same since her granddaughter, Rachel, was reported missing last year. I wonder whatever happened to that girl. What in the world would possess an 18-year-old girl to run away while she's visiting her grandparents for the summer?"

"We don't know that she did run away," Dad said matter-of-factly.

Mom's voice became loud and shrill. "What? Well, of course she ran away. What else could've happened to her? My goodness!"

With his back to them, Greg rolled his eyes and sighed deeply. "Bye."

Later, down by the lake, with his cell phone safely clipped to his waistband, Greg stood on the wooden plank pier, casting his yellow surface plug into a patch of lily pads, while keeping a watchful eye on the twins. Timmy and Tommy were standing in the shallow water next to the pier, racing their boats. The yellow, bug-shaped lure landed in the water with a soft PLOOP! Greg waited until all the ripples vanished, then he jerked his pole up—just a little—causing the plug to twitch ever so slightly. While waiting for the new batch of ripples to disappear, he scanned the saw-toothed horizon that surrounded Mink Lake. So many pine trees, he thought, taking in the scenic view. Must be thousands of 'em.

Even though he and his family had been vacationing here for the last two years, he never got used to the splendor, the beauty, and the tranquility of the wilderness. For here he could get away from it all, get away from Dad, who,

Greg thought, was encroaching on Greg's lifestyle with each passing minute. Why can't Dad be cool like Mom? he wondered. After all, isn't a soon-to-be 18-year-old boy—man—supposed to be treated like a man? If not now, then when?

He cupped his hand over his eyes, squinting against the July evening sun; marveling at the pine-studded mound that seemed to be floating in the middle of the 1500 acre lake. Even Tucker Island is overgrown with pines, he thought. He took a deep breath, filling his nostrils with rich pine scent. Hearing footsteps behind him, he turned and wrinkled his nose at the sight of Jenny on the pier.

An explosion in the water about 30 yards away startled him. He glanced in the direction of the noise just in time to see a bass—a very big bass—fall back into the water, crashing through the lily pads with the yellow lure hanging from its mouth. Greg jerked the rod back, setting the hook deep into the bass's jaw. "I got one! I got one!" he yelled, his adrenaline pumping.

The twins whooped and hollered with uncontrollable excitement. Their toy boats zigged and zagged every which way in their distraction.

Spook raced up and down the shoreline, barking happily at the little boats that zipped back and forth in the shallow water, taunting him.

During the ruckus, and while he was wrestling his bass in from the lily pads, Greg noticed two elderly fishermen sitting in their aluminum boat about a hundred yards away, casting to the pads. "Might as well get the hell out of here," one them snapped, pulling up the anchor. "Too much damn noise around here."

Spook barked and barked, his tongue dangling out the side of his mouth, his tail swishing frantically.

"They oughta put a muzzle on that mutt," the other fisherman snarled, pulling the starter cord on his outboard motor. "How you supposed to catch any fish around here with all that barking going on?"

I'm not having any trouble catching any, Greg thought, grinning with delight, trying to work the bass from the weed bed.

Within seconds, the boat disappeared behind a pine-studded peninsula that jutted into the lake several hundred yards away.

Even when the boat was no longer in sight, Greg could still hear the old men crabbing and cussing about Spook, their voices clearly audible above the muffled growl of the motor.

Good riddance, Greg thought. Now there's more fish for me! He concentrated on reeling in his bass. From the start, he had expected to feel the usual tug of a one or two-pound bass, in which case the fight would have been over in just a few seconds. But this was not the usual low-scale fight of a smallsize bass. This bass was huge—much larger than what he was accustomed to catching in Mink Lake—and it fought accordingly. "Jeez," he said, amazed, "this thing is really fighting. Must be at least four or five pounds."

"Oh, boy!" Timmy cried, water dripping off his freckled nose. "It's a big one!"

"Gweg caught a big one!" Tommy chimed in.

The bass lunged suddenly into deeper water, bulldozing its way through a tangle of lily pads, weaving the fishing line through a thick maze of underwater stems.

Greg held on tight, feeding out just enough line to keep it from snapping.

Suddenly the bass broke water, flipping itself into the air, red gills flashing, spraying flecks of water and bits of weeds everywhere. When it fell back into the water, it made a diagonal run away from the lily pads and into open water.

Greg's heart jumped into his throat, his mouth hanging open in shocked disbelief at the size of the fish. "That's not a four or five pounder," he gushed. "That thing's at least 10 or 12 pounds! Did you see the size of that thing?"

"Big deal—so you caught a fish," Jenny said. "Watch him get away."

"No way! I've got him now!" Greg cried, cranking in the line, his adrenaline racing like wildfire. "He's got nowhere to hide, nowhere to run." Judging by the dwindling drag on the line, he knew the bass was tiring. "Won't be long now," he said proudly, cranking the reel with increasing ease. "He's mine. Come on, sugar. Come to Daddy."

Abruptly, the line went limp.

Greg stumbled backwards from the sudden lack of pressure on the line. "What?" he cried. "What happened? What the heck happened?" He reeled in the slack line that was now minus not only the bass, but also the yellow plug. "I don't get it. That thing was on there, and he was on there good. Damn!"

"What happened, Gweg?" Timmy asked, looking up at his older brother through soulful eyes. He was still standing in three feet of water, clutching his remote control box to his chest.

"It got away!" Tommy shrieked, exasperated, waving a tight, little fist at his twin. "Can't you see?"

"Nice going, Greg," Jenny said tauntingly, her smirk a mile wide. She was lying on the pier behind Greg, her slim, oil-drenched body sprawled out on top of an orange beach towel. "I told you he'd get away." Her hair was drawn back into a ponytail, and Greg noticed with disgust that she was chewing on the end of it.

Timmy's toy boat smacked into one of the posts at the front of the pier, bouncing off harmlessly.

From the shoreline, Spook spotted the toy and dashed along the pier, leaping over Jenny, brushing past Greg, and coming to an abrupt stop at the very edge, barking frantically at the buzzing toy.

"Shut up, Spook!" Greg yelled, annoyed. He returned his attention to Jenny munching on her ponytail. "That's gross," he shouted above Spook's barking, disgusted.

"Not as gross as your zit face," she shot back.

The remark stung him, wounded him, deflated him. The disappointment he felt over the loss of his big bass quickly swelled into hatred toward his sister. He wanted to hit her, make her hurt back. Why not, he thought. I've got a black belt in karate. Let the stupid brat have it. She deserves it. But he knew it was out of the question. He wouldn't really hit her. When they were younger, and their fighting had been severe and nonstop, Dad had warned him to never hit a girl because it was one of the most unmanly things a guy could do. After years of preaching—and warning—the rule was well ingrained.

So he took his anger out on Spook instead, who was still standing at the end of the pier, barking at Timmy's boat. "Shut up, mutt!" he yelled, pushing the dog off the pier with his foot. "All you do is bark. Go lie down!"

Spook fell unharmed into the lake with a loud splash. But his barking never stopped. Now he partly swam, partly leaped in the shallow water, chasing the colorful toy boats circling round and round in the water.

"Don't take it out on the dog, zit face," Jenny sneered, chomping on her thick ponytail.

Spook's barking grew louder, more frantic.

"You should've locked him up like I told you to when I

first came down here," she went on. "I told you to lock him up, didn't I?" She was obviously basking in his disappointment over the loss of his bass and his subsequent tantrum.

Spook's barking turned shrill, wild.

Annoyed, Greg ignored the barking and glared at Jenny, his muscles tense with rage. "Who do you think you're talking to, you little twerp. You don't tell me what to do—ever! Understand? If you want that dog locked up so bad, *you* lock him up, Toyota Face. You wonder why you can't get a boyfriend—you got enough chrome on your mouth to scare *any* guy away." Oooh, it felt so good to tell her off. But more than good, he felt guilty. Deep in the back of his mind, he realized that *this* was why Dad didn't treat him like a man. He knew that shoving Spook into the lake, screaming at Jenny, calling her names, and making fun of her braces was the very behavior that Dad was always scolding him for and telling him to grow up and act like a man. Nice going, Greg, he thought, feeling remorse. You did it again.

Spook's barking turned fierce, maniacal, but Greg ignored it, still glaring at Jenny.

An enormous splash in the water behind him distracted Greg momentarily, but he kept his eyes glued on Jenny, trying to let go of his anger. Suddenly aware of the fishing rod he was squeezing and twisting in his hands, he took a deep breath and made a conscious effort to relax his grip.

The barking grew louder, shriller.

"At least I don't have a stupid flattop haircut to go with your ugly zit face," Jenny fired. Apparently she had no intention of backing off.

The raving barking grew still louder, shriller.

Still ignoring it, Greg calmly envisioned himself throwing Jenny in the lake and holding her obnoxious, bratty, little face underwater until it turned a wonderful shade of blue.

The barking was now wildly insane.

Suddenly Greg realized that Spook's barking was anything but normal. He whipped his head around and faced the lake, just as the twins screamed. He searched his brothers' faces, trying to determine in a split-second whether the screams were cries of joy ... or shrieks of terror.

And then he saw it—a pair of flesh-colored tendrils with black speckles, fully 10 feet long, just barely break the surface on either side of Spook. An enormous dark shadow lurked just beneath the water directly behind the dog. Greg dropped his fishing pole in the lake, his eyes wide with shock, his mouth dangling open. "What the—"

The water beneath Spook appeared to split open, and a tremendous sucking sound erupted from the dark, watery slit.

Spook threw his head up, holding it high out of the water, his thick neck straining, his big brown eyes bulging from their sockets. An earsplitting yowl escaped from his trembling snout and echoed clear around the lake.

Then, in a fraction of a second, with one violent thrust, Spook was gone.

Greg felt his heart jump in his throat. Fear gripped every muscle in his body. He was frozen in place, unable to move, unable to speak, his knees turning to rubber.

The water where Spook disappeared smoothed over, and not a trace of the dog remained—no blood, no fur, nothing ... not even a ripple.

For a moment that felt like an eternity, Greg stood on the edge of the pier, staring at the calm, flat water, shocked beyond belief, an overwhelming feeling of doom washing over him.

A scream from Timmy shattered the spell.

Greg snapped his head in the direction of the scream,

and his heart exploded with a new fear—a cold, gut-wrenching fear that shook his insides, making him weak and dizzy.

Beneath the water a few yards away, the huge dark shadow moved steadily toward Timmy. It was easily 15 or 20 feet long and perhaps six feet wide. Timmy was standing in only three-and-a-half-feet of water—seemingly too shallow for something as huge as the shadowy figure to move in.

But it is moving, Greg thought, horrified. "TIMMY! IT'S COMING AT YOU! GET OUT OF THE WATER! TIMMY!" he screamed, clenching his fists.

He heard Jenny gasp behind him. "Oh, my God! Greg! What is it?" she asked, clinging to his arm, panic in her voice. "Oh, my God! It's going after Timmy! Greg! Do something! Oh, my God! TIM-MEEEEEEEEEEEEEEEEEEEE!"

Jenny's scream triggered a scream from Tommy, who was standing in three feet of water at the end of the pier. Lunging for safety, he tossed his remote control box onto the pier, then scrambled up onto the plank deck. Flinging his skinny arms around Jenny's waist, he buried his head in her stomach and sobbed. "Timmy's in twouble. Timmy's in twouble. Pwease save Timmy!"

Timmy stood frozen in the water, staring at the approaching shadow, a look of utter confusion on his freckled face.

"Do something, Greg!" Jenny screamed. "For God's sake, do something!" The shadow moved in closer, no more than 10 feet away now. Timmy's face paled, but still he didn't budge.

"TIMMY!" Greg screamed. "GET OUT OF THERE!" Jump! Greg told himself. Jump in and save your little brother, for Christ's sake! Do it! Now!

Eight feet and closing.

Greg's mind was numb with fear. Panic gripped his very

soul. "TIMMY!" Save him. For God's sake, save him. Please! Oh, please! Jump in and save him! Save him! Oh, God! Save him!

Seven feet.

I can't. Too big. It's too damn big! I can't!

Six feet.

"TIMMY!"

CHAPTER 2

Greg saw it was dangerously close now, its huge form dark and menacing. Timmy remained frozen in place, his eyes wide with terror, glued to the approaching creature.

From the corner of his eye, Greg briefly caught sight of the toy boats buzzing toward one another, completely uncontrolled, the colorful plastic hulls skimming the surface at full speed.

The monstrous shadow glided toward Timmy with the greatest of ease, like a deadly torpedo, sliding silently, stealthily beneath the surface, only a few feet away from the intended target.

Greg felt his stomach twist and churn, pulling tighter and tighter, his heart hammering. Blood rushed to his head, surging inside his veins, pounding in his ears. His eardrums ached and threatened to explode from Jenny's deafening screams. Do something! he thought, struggling against blinding fear. Save him! "TIMMY!" he screamed, digging his nails into his palms. "MOVE, TIMMY! "MOVE!"

Long, fleshy tendrils broke the surface, stretching flat and heavy on top of the water, like thick power cables, sinister-looking and chock-full of deadly danger.

Timmy's face faded to a ghastly white, his lips blue and

quivering. He curled his hands protectively beneath his chin, his eyes bulging, his body trembling. He remained glued to the spot, his frail, freckled frame sticking up out of the water, like a carrot about to be plucked from the garden.

A sick feeling of doom exploded inside of Greg, and tears of desperation welled in his eyes. "Tim—" His voice cracked around a lump that throbbed deep in his throat.

The creature was only three feet away now. The water in front of Timmy appeared to boil and swirl. The snake-like tendrils were only inches away, stretched out on either side of the boy like long, treacherous arms about to embrace him.

Jenny's screams made Greg's flesh crawl, and triggered further screaming from Tommy.

Only two feet away.

"GREG! FOR GOD'S SAKE, DO SOMETHING!" Jenny shrieked.

Greg's mind whirled in panic, his heart banging furiously against his chest.

Only eighteen inches away.

Desperate, horror-stricken, and not knowing what else to do, Greg snatched up Tommy's remote control box on the pier and cranked the dial, steering Tommy's boat directly at Timmy's boat.

Then ...

CRASH!

The toy boats had zoomed into the remaining gap between Timmy and the creature and crashed head-on with tremendous force, spraying Timmy with shards of red and yellow plastic.

The creature veered sharply to one side, turning away from Timmy at the last possible moment in one fluid motion, apparently scared off by the noise of the collision. Its movement was so swift, so instantaneous, it appeared to be mounted on a mechanical pivot. As it darted away, its enormous tail crashed into Timmy, sweeping him off his feet, plunging him underwater.

Greg sprang from the pier, diving into the lake, his lean, muscular body piercing the surface like a bullet. Seconds later, he resurfaced, cradling Timmy in his arms.

Timmy's limp body dangled freely, his face wracked with stark terror, his bulging eyes staring blankly. Water sputtered from his gaping mouth. "Oh, my God!" Jenny shrieked. "Is he all right? Is he hurt?"

Greg held him above the waist-high water and carried him back to the pier. "I think he's in shock," Greg said, handing him up to Jenny.

She quickly wrapped him in her beach towel, then snuggled him in her arms. "He's shaking like a leaf." She held his face against her own, stroking the back of his head. He started crying. "Shh. It's okay, honey," Jenny said softly. "You're all right. Shh. It's okay, honey. It's okay."

Greg climbed up onto the pier, his clothes and shoes dripping wet.

"Timmy's gonna die! Timmy's gonna die!" Tommy sobbed, throwing his arms around Greg's waist. Looking up at his older brother, his face twisted with grief, tears streaming down his freckled cheeks, he tried to speak, his voice choked with sobs. "Gweg … is Timmy gonna die now?"

Watching Timmy tremble, seeing the little boy suffer in agonizing terror, then watching Tommy sob, his little heart breaking in two, Greg fought an overwhelming urge to burst into tears. He hated himself, despised himself for allowing Timmy to come so close to death. I'm a coward, he thought, the lump in his throat doubling. I should've jumped in right away. Shouldn't have waited like that. Would *Dad* have waited? Timmy could've been killed! His shame was so heavy, he wanted to die himself.

"Is he Gweg? Is he gonna die?"

Greg felt hot tears nipping at his eyes, stinging, burning. Kneeling down, he embraced Tommy, comforting him. "No," he said, trying desperately to squeeze his voice past the swelling lump in his throat. "He's not gonna die. It's all right. Timmy's okay." Feeling unsure of himself, he looked up at Jenny, gazing inquisitively at her through his tears.

"He seems okay," she said, still stroking the back of Timmy's head. "But I think you're right—he might be in shock. We should call for help." Her tone was matter-of-factly, her manner cool, calm. "We have to report this to the police."

Another pang of guilt swept over Greg. Here he was, the big, strong brother who was supposed to be in charge of everyone, watching over them, protecting them. Instead, he let his little brother almost die right under his nose. And then he cried about it like some helpless, immature baby. And here's his sister—his small, physically weak sister— who was obviously showing greater self-control over the situation than he was. She's got more guts than me, he thought, brushing tears away with his hand. *I'm* the one with a black belt in karate. *I'm* the one who's supposed to be tough. *I'm* the one who's supposed to be in control. He dabbed at more tears, glancing at Jenny. She'll never let me live *this* one down.

"Well?" Jenny asked. "Are you gonna call someone or what?"

Greg reached for his cell phone, but it was no longer clipped to his waistband. "My phone's missing!" he cried, searching the pier deck. But it was nowhere to be found. "Must've fallen off when I jumped in the lake."

"Well, don't even *think* of going back in the water to find it," Jenny said.

"Even if I did find it," Greg said, "it wouldn't work now anyhow—being soaking wet."

"So what do we do now?" Jenny asked. "Thanks to Dad, we don't have a phone in the cabin, and we don't have a car."

Greg's mind whirled and fluttered. Think damn it! Think! He felt like cursing Dad, for it was Dad's stupid idea to have no house phone, no radio, and no TV at the cabin. Tired of the civilized rat race back home in Illinois, Dad wanted to isolate the family from the turbulent real world while on vacation. Greg could still remember Dad's words from two years ago when they had first purchased the cabin: "Just think, we've got no neighbors, no phone, no radio, no TV, and no newspaper or mail delivery. And the nearest town is ten miles away. We've got something that most people will never get to experience ... total seclusion. We're all alone in the north woods. Now we can have real peace and quiet."

The twins were too small to care then, but Greg, Mom, and Jenny had all objected to Dad's absurd idea of life with no phone or TV. But their objection had been in vain—as usual. Once Dad set down "the law," that was that. There was no getting around it.

Nice going, Dad, Greg thought bitterly. Now what are we supposed to do in case of a *real* emergency? We're stranded here, with no house phone, no cell phone, and no car. And Mrs. Tucker is only a nurse—a retired nurse.

"Like I said—what do we do now?" Jenny asked sharply.

Greg took a deep breath, then talked slowly—very slowly—so his voice wouldn't crack. "The nearest neighbor is six miles away, Jen. And it'll be dark soon. The only thing we can do now is row over to Tucker Island."

"Now?" Jenny asked, shocked. "You gotta be kidding!" She nodded at the small wooden rowboat that was stored upside down on the beach. "You expect us to get in that little boat and row it across the lake with that *thing* in the water? You're crazy! No way! We're not going out there." Still holding Timmy with one arm, she slipped her other arm around Tommy and pulled him close. "What *was* that thing, anyway?"

Greg faced her, his temper rising. "I'm not sure, but it looked like a giant catfish. Now you listen to me, Jenny. I'm still in charge here—like it or not—and Timmy needs help. And the only help around is the Tuckers'." He walked over to the rowboat, flipped it over, shoved it into the water, and tied it to the pier. "Now take the twins and get your butt in the boat. I have to run up to the cabin for the oars and life jackets. I'll be right back." He started sprinting toward the cabin when Jenny asked, "A giant what?"

"Catfish, Jenny," he called over his shoulder.

"What were those long fleshy things by its mouth?"

Greg rolled his eyes. "Whiskers, Jenny. Those were its whiskers. All catfish have whiskers. Just like a cat. That's why they call them catfish. Now get in the boat."

Inside the cabin, Greg scrambled about, gathering oars and life jackets. He loaded his arms with the bulky equipment, clutching the items to his chest, partially obstructing his vision. Then, in his haste to leave, he tripped over something on the floor next to the door. "Darn it!" he cried, crashing into the screen door, dropping the life jackets, and piercing the screen with an oar. As he picked up the scattered jackets, he discovered what had tripped him: the large pail of Chlordane Dad has set by the door earlier. He must've forgot it, he thought, annoyed. Nice going, Dad. Another swift move. Thanks for almost breaking my neck with your stupid pesticides. Then, out loud, he said, "Here's another swift move ...."

He deliberately kicked the metal pail, leaving a dent in its side.

Back at the pier, with everyone safely inside the boat, and wearing their life jackets, Greg untied the rowboat and cast off. His eyes scanned the lake, noting the considerable distance between them and Tucker Island. That's a lot of water to cross, he thought, the sick, dreadful feeling in his gut growing more intense. I wish I had my pistol.

CHAPTER 3

An evening calm had settled over Mink Lake, its surface smooth and flat, like a piece of glass. Halfway across the lake, Greg thought he spotted the monster trailing behind them. "Lie down on the bottom of the boat!" he ordered the others, expecting an attack any second. Clutching an oar as a weapon, he stood guard over Jenny and the twins huddled at his feet. With his eyes squinted, he searched the water, his heart pounding.

But the attack never came.

"Do you see it?" Jenny cried, holding her head down, her arms clamped protectively around the twins.

"No," Greg said, puzzled ... and relieved. "It's gone. Where'd it go? I could've sworn I saw it." But now he wondered if he had seen the giant catfish after all. Maybe it was only the long, murky shadows cast in the water by the sliver of sun peering above distant pine trees that he had seen. Either way, he wasn't about to waste another moment thinking about it. He resumed rowing—hard and fast—trying to beat nightfall.

When he arrived at Tucker Island, he tied the small wooden rowboat to the Tuckers' pier, sighing relief. As he helped Jenny and the twins out of the boat, he noticed

Timmy's color had come back. "He looks better already," Greg said, taking Timmy out of Jenny's arms. "But I still better carry him up to the house."

The Tuckers' house was a two-story, rustic log cabin, nestled on the four-acre island in a dense forest of pine, aspen, oak, birch, and maple.

Walking up the stone steps to the front porch, Greg marveled at the thick, rough-hewn logs, expertly cut and fitted, and recalled Dad telling him that Mr. Tucker had built the house himself some fifty years ago. I bet his dad was proud of him, he thought, ringing the doorbell. Whose dad *wouldn't* be proud if their son built an entire house all by himself? His brow furrowed. Mine!

The heavy plank door creaked open, and a little old lady who could've passed for Mrs. Santa Claus—button nose, rosy cheeks, hair tied in a bun, wire rim glasses perched halfway down her nose, and a short, plump figure—stood in the doorway. "Children!" she cried, throwing her hands in the air. "What a wonderful surprise! Come in! Come in!" Her voice was warm, cheery, sincere, but her face clouded suddenly when she noticed Timmy in Greg's arms.

"Hello, Mrs. Tucker," Greg said, stepping sideways through the doorway, careful not to bang Timmy's head on the doorjamb, Jenny and Tommy following. "Timmy's had an accident. We think he's in shock."

"Oh, dear!" Mrs. Tucker cried, clasping her hands together, her cheeks growing redder. "What happened? Oh, dear! Here, put him on the sofa," she said, ushering them into the living room. She ran to the foot of the stairs in the hallway that separated the living room from the dining room. "Andy! Come down quick! It's the Nelson children. There's been an accident!" Then she bustled over to the sofa, leaned over Timmy, picked up his wrist, and checked his pulse. "What happened?"

she asked, staring intently at Greg, her eyes wide with alarm, her cheeks deeply flushed now.

Before Greg could explain, Mr. Tucker shuffled into the room, a look of bewilderment on his face. Mrs. Tucker may have looked like Mrs. Santa Claus, but *Mr.* Tucker bore no resemblance at all to *Mr.* Santa Claus. He was tall, thin, and bony. His gray hair was short and bristly, his face wrinkled and beardless. He walked with the unsure gait of an old man, deliberate and unsteady, as though he were struggling to maintain his balance with every footstep. "What's all the commotion about?" he asked, his voice old and raspy. "What hap—?"

"Thank goodness!" Mrs. Tucker interrupted, examining Timmy's pupils. "He's not in shock, but he looks like he's had the daylights scared out of him."

"He did, Mrs. Tucker," Greg said. "Believe me ...he did."

"Well, you'll have to tell us all about it, but first I want to get him some warm milk. It'll help him relax."

"Mrs. Tuck-or," Tommy chimed in, "can I have some milk, too?"

Mrs. Tucker smiled warmly, her eyes twinkling. "Of course, Tommy," she said, gently rubbing his fuzzy head. "And how about some cookies, too?"

"Oh, boy!" Tommy cried. "Cookies!" He went to the sofa and put his hand on Timmy's forehead. "Don't worwy, Timmy. You'll be all wight af-tor you have your cookies."

Timmy's eyes widened at the mere mention of the word.

Mrs. Tucker chuckled. To Greg and Jenny she said, "How about some soda and chips?"

"Sounds good," Greg said. "Thank you."

"Thank you, Mrs. Tucker," Jenny said shyly.

"I'll be right back." On the way to the kitchen, she said, "Build us a fire, Andy. This night air is damp and chilly."

Later, in the cozy comfort of the Tuckers' rustic living room, Greg told them about the attack on Spook and Timmy. He explained in detail what the creature had looked like, and how it had vanished just as quickly as it had appeared.

Mrs. Tucker was sitting on the sofa, listening intently, Timmy fast asleep on her lap. Jenny was sitting next to her, sipping soda from a can.

Mr. Tucker was in his wicker rocking chair next to the stone fireplace, gently rocking Tommy to sleep.

When Greg finished his story, the Tuckers sat in silence, staring at each other, confused, their faces cast in doubt. Only the soft crackling of the fire and the methodic squeaking of the rocking chair could be heard.

Having told his story, recalling the dreadful events, Greg was glad—damn glad—to be in the warmth and safety of this room that glowed with firelight. He looked up at the vaulted ceiling with its knotty pine boards, supported by thick wooden beams, and exhaled deeply. For the first time all evening, he began to relax. Soaking in the coziness of the room, he let himself scan the familiar decor: knotty pine paneling, plank flooring, an oval braided rug in front of the sofa, a mounted bear head above the fireplace, another one over the doorway that led into the hallway, and a mounted deer head hanging above the front door. He was puzzled when his eyes rested upon an oak gun cabinet in the corner next to the hallway entrance. Funny ... I don't remember seeing *that* before, he thought. Must be new. He began to walk toward it to get a closer look at the twelve guns lined up, standing erect, behind the double glass doors, when Mr. Tucker's voice stopped him.

"I know you saw *something* out there, Greg," Mr. Tucker said, stroking his chin. "But a giant catfish?"

"Incredible!" Mrs. Tucker said, still staring at her husband. "I've never heard of such a thing."

"Nor *seen* such a thing," Mr. Tucker added.

"No, it was definitely a giant catfish, Mr. Tucker," Greg said. "I know it sounds crazy, but believe me ... I know what I saw. Jenny and the twins saw it, too."

From the double pockets on his red flannel shirt, Mr. Tucker removed a pipe and a black leather pouch filled with tobacco. "I'll tell ya something, Greg. I've been living on this island for more than fifty years, and I ain't never seen no giant catfish in this lake. Hell, the biggest I've seen was only forty-seven pounds, and that was many years ago. With all this modern day pollution, you'd be lucky to see one *half* that big nowadays." He dug his pipe into the pouch, filling the bowl with brown, crinkled tobacco, then tamped it with a large, bony thumb before lighting it. A wispy cloud of blue-gray smoke hung in the air above his head, filling the room with a rich, sweet aroma. "Besides, if there *was* a giant catfish out there, how come we ain't seen nor heard about it till now? How you suppose something that big could've stayed hidden all these years?"

Greg felt exasperated, frustrated. "Okay, look ... I know it sounds unbelievable, but I'm telling you the truth. I swear to God it was a giant catfish. We're lucky Timmy's still alive. Ask Jenny—she was there."

Jenny sat in silence, her eyes glued to the fireplace, her stare deep, intense, as though she were mesmerized by the flames.

Silence—save the crackling of the fire and the squeaking of the chair.

Mr. Tucker puffed on his pipe, rocking gently, one arm cradling Tommy, who was now fast asleep on his lap. "It could've been a musky," he said thoughtfully. "Ya know, muskies get pretty big up here—fifty or sixty pounds. "Now that's a mighty big fish—in any lake."

Greg felt himself becoming annoyed with Mr. Tucker, his anger smoldering. I'm not going to lose my temper, he thought. He's just an old man—a harmless old man who was kind enough to take us in. He looked at Jenny and the twins. His flicker of anger was quickly extinguished. "But this thing had *whiskers,* Mr. Tucker—ten or twelve feet long. That was no *damn* musky." Oops! He slipped—he didn't mean to swear. Too late.

Shocked, Mr. Tucker's rocking stopped abruptly, as he stared incredulously at Greg, his mouth hanging open, pipe dangling precariously. A moment later, he resumed rocking and puffing on his pipe, his stare shifting to Mrs. Tucker.

Mrs. Tucker fidgeted with her glasses: taking them off, looking at them, blowing on them, then putting them on again. "Well, you're safe here, anyway," she said with a strained smile. "And whatever it was you saw out there, I think you should report it to the sheriff first thing in the morning."

Suddenly Jenny spoke, her voice soft, almost a whisper, her eyes still glued to the fireplace. "Whatever it was, it was big enough to eat our dog—all hundred pounds of him." She shuddered, never breaking her gaze.

Mrs. Tucker put her arm around her, drawing her close. "We're sorry, honey. That's terrible. But don't worry—everything will be all right. It's okay. You're all safe now. We'll get to the bottom of this."

"We ain't got no phone here, Greg," Mr. Tucker said, relighting his pipe. "They don't run phone lines or power lines to the island. We're on a generator here. Ain't got one of them newfangled cell phones, either. But I got an old pickup truck parked at the public landing over at Turner's Point—

you know, over there on the peninsula. You can take my speedboat to the landing, and from there you can take my truck into town to see Sheriff Clifford."

Greg felt ashamed of himself for having been annoyed with the old man. He's on *my* side, he thought. I'm my own worst enemy. "Thanks, Mr. Tucker. I appreciate it."

"You kids are welcome to stay as long as you like," Mrs. Tucker said.

"Thank you, Mrs. Tucker," Greg said. "Under the circumstances, I *will* keep them here until Mom and Dad get back. But don't worry, we'll stay out of your way."

"Don't be silly," Mrs. Tucker scolded. "You kids are no bother at all. We're glad to have your company. You just make yourselves at home."

Mr. Tucker set his pipe in the ashtray on the small table next to his rocking chair. Eyeing his wristwatch, he said, "What say we put these little ones to bed now, Ma?"

"Dear me, yes," Mrs. Tucker replied, looking at the twins and smiling. "The poor little dears. It must've been quite a shock for both of them."

"Here ... we'll take them," Greg volunteered, gently lifting Timmy from Mrs. Tucker's lap, careful not to wake him. He kissed Timmy on his forehead, grateful that the twins were safe.

"There's two spare bedrooms upstairs at the end of the hall," Mrs. Tucker said. "The one on the left has a double bed, so you can put the twins in there. The one on the right has a twin bed, so Jenny can sleep in there. I'm afraid you'll have to sleep down here on the sofa, Greg."

"That's no problem," Greg said. "No problem at all. Thank you." As he headed toward the stairs, he stopped in front of the gun cabinet, eyeing the dozen polished guns. "Is this new? I don't remember seeing it before."

"No, it's not new," Mr. Tucker replied, getting up from his rocking chair, handing Tommy over to Jenny. "I've had it for years down in the basement, but the dampness down there is causing 'em to rust. So I hired a couple of local boys in town, had 'em come over one day and bring the darn thing upstairs. I just spent all day yesterday, cleaning and oiling 'em."

"Wow," Greg said, admiring the small arsenal. "You got some real nice rifles and shotguns in there."

"Yeah ... most of 'em is still in pretty good shape, too." Mr. Tucker opened the glass doors, reached inside, and removed a particularly mean-looking piece. "This here is my newest addition," he said, beaming. "It's an AK-47 assault rifle. I got it from a guy in town who was running an ad in the paper, trying to sell it. She's a real beauty—and only three hundred bucks!"

"An AK-47?" Greg asked, astonished. "What do you need *that* for? I mean—what kind of animals do you hunt with it? Bears?"

"No, no," Mr. Tucker answered, chuckling. "I don't *need* it for anything."

"Amen," Mrs. Tucker quipped, rolling her eyes.

Mr. Tucker ignored her. "You can't hunt anything with it—it's illegal. Besides ... there wouldn't be any sport in it—this thing's fully automatic. Just squeeze the trigger, and she'll shoot thirty rounds in seconds. And ... she can shoot holes right through steel pipe, concrete blocks, wooden posts ... you name it!" He rubbed the wooden stock with his shirttail, polishing it. "No, I don't *need* it for anything—I just like collecting guns, that's all."

"Geez," Greg said, staring in awe at the gun. "That's a deadly weapon in the hands of a maniac."

"She's a deadly weapon in the hands of *anyone*," Mr.

Tucker corrected. "All ya gotta do is slip the magazine into this slot here, pull the lever back to cock it, aim, and fire. Then ... hold on to your hat, 'cause she kicks like a son-of-a-gun! Uh, no pun intended. Heh, heh, heh."

"Do you keep these things loaded?" Jenny asked. She was holding Tommy, who was sound asleep, his thumb stuck in his mouth.

"No, no," Mr. Tucker said, his tone suddenly serious. "No need to keep 'em loaded. That's much too dangerous. I keep the bullets locked up in the bottom compartment there." He pointed to the bottom section of the gun cabinet, which consisted of two small oak doors, trimmed with brass handles, brass hinges, and a brass keyhole. "And don't worry ... I always keep them doors locked. So it'll be safe with the twins."

"I wish I could go bear hunting sometime," Greg said, staring at one of the bolt-action rifles, dreaming of thrills and adventure. "Talk about excitement! That would be a blast!"

"Well, I wish I could take ya sometime," Mr. Tucker said sincerely. "But I'm afraid my hunting days are over. I'm too old to tramp through the woods, looking for bears ... or having them looking for *me!* Heh, heh."

"Bear hunting!" Jenny interrupted. "Greg? Bear hunting? Excuse me, but doesn't bear hunting require a small degree of ... *guts?*" As she was leaving the room, carrying Tommy, she turned in the doorway, looked at Greg, and smirked.

Greg blushed violently as he glared at her, his upper lip quivering.

Mr. Tucker seemed to have not heard the sarcastic remark, for he resumed his conversation right where he had left off, as though he had never been interrupted in the first place. Either he hadn't heard it, or he simply chose not to acknowledge it.

Greg was grateful, either way.

"Now I just kinda sit back and look at my guns, admire 'em, clean 'em, oil 'em. I enjoy 'em the same way some people enjoy collecting dolls, or stamps, or coins. And someday when I'm gone, my son in Ohio will get 'em. I hope he'll enjoy 'em as much as I have."

Mr. Tucker's face clouded suddenly. "He ain't got no boys of his own. Just a girl—one girl. So when he's gone, he'll be leaving 'em all to my granddaughter, Rachel." He fell silent at the mention of Rachel's name. His eyes narrowed as he stared intently at the row of guns, his mind a million miles away. Then, still in a daze, he whispered softly, barely audible: "Where are you, Rachel? What ever happened to you? Where did you go?"

Greg saw tears brimming in the old man's eyes. Poor guy, he thought, suddenly feeling uncomfortable. How do you console an old, tired man whose only grandchild has disappeared?

He recalled the details surrounding the mystery. Rachel had been visiting the Tuckers last summer, just as she had done every summer with her parents for the last several years. But last summer had been different—special to Rachel— because last summer her parents decided not to make the trip with her. They had given her permission to make the trip all alone in her own car. As Mrs. Tucker had told Mom, it was the snipping of the "parental apron strings," releasing her from the rigid boundaries of childhood and into the unrestricted realm of womanhood.

Rachel had been ecstatic over her newfound freedom and independence. But only two days after her arrival at Tucker Island, she mysteriously disappeared without a trace. Sheriff Clifford had ruled her disappearance as merely a common runaway because there had been "no shred of evidence to indicate foul play." Her car, a white, two-door Ford, which she'd left parked at the public landing, was also gone. And the Tuckers' speedboat had been found docked at the public landing, indicating that Rachel had simply left on her own free will—but without saying goodbye to her grandparents?

Greg shrugged, and carried Timmy upstairs.

CHAPTER 4

A light fog hovered above the lake, swirling and coiling lazily beneath the early morning sun. Somewhere deep inside the thin, gray mist, a loon shattered the stillness with its mournful cry. Its call was immediately answered by another loon hidden in the soup, its shrill laughter erupting from the opposite end of the lake.

Having showered, but still dressed in yesterday's clothes—jeans, T-shirt, and sneakers—Greg shivered against the chilly air as he climbed into Mr. Tucker's speedboat. He slipped the key in the ignition and switched on the 140 horsepower motor, gritting his teeth against the sudden noise. He had been extra careful not to wake the others, having tiptoed through the house, softly closing doors behind him. The Tuckers were old and needed their sleep, and the twins were plumb tuckered out after yesterday's frightening ordeal. And Jenny—he recalled her cutting remark last night about him not having any guts. The hell with Jenny, he thought, opening the throttle.

The motor roared as the boat sped away, slicing through fog and water, a roiling, white-capped wake trailing behind.

On his way to the public landing, taking in the sights of the northwestern woods at daybreak, filling his lungs with the fresh, clean air, he thought of how ironic it was that such a beautiful lake could harbor a giant, man-eating monster. What's more, how long had it been living here? Where had it come from? How could it be that no one else ever saw it or heard about it before? Why him? Why *his* family? Why Spook? Poor Spook. He had been a good dog, loyal to the family, always protective of them. "I loved that dog." Greg wiped a tear from his eye. "Poor thing never knew what hit him."

At the public landing, Greg docked the speedboat, then hopped into Mr. Tucker's pickup truck. The truck—a green ancient '67 Ford—was rusted, dented, scratched, and fenderless. A crack in the windshield stretched from the upper left corner to the lower right. Greg slipped the key into the ignition and was surprised when the engine actually turned over. "Way to go!" he cried, bouncing on the cloth-covered seat. A cloud of dust billowed from the torn fabric, engulfing him. He coughed and waved the dust away from his face. "Can't get worse than this," he said, shifting gears. "What a wreck!" He pulled out onto the sand road that would lead him into the town of Wolverine, ten miles away.

About two miles from the landing, the truck began to pop, chug, and rattle. The vehicle slowed to a crawl, and just as Greg steered to the side of the road, it died completely with one final POP! As he climbed out of the cab, steam burst from beneath the hood, hissing vehemently.

"Oh, that's just great!" he cried, kicking the left front tire, and then the hood popped up, releasing a final puff of steam. "Fantastic! Now what?"

He cupped his hand above his brow, squinting against the July sun, scouting the road north and south. But there was nothing to see but miles and miles of sand road, lined with acres and acres of pine trees. "Some vacation *this* is turning out to be." He kicked the tire again, and it popped, then hissed until it was completely flat. "Wonderful."

A pair of crows landed noisily in the pine boughs directly above him, scolding him with their loud, incessant cawing. CAW! CAW! CAW! CAW! CAW!

Disgusted and annoyed, Greg looked up at the large black birds, their sleek, shiny feathers glistening in the sunlight. "Ah, shut up!" He scooped up a handful of sand at his feet and flung it at the pesky intruders.

The crows burst from their roost, soaring high into the sky above the road. Then, with indignation and defiance, they swooped down one last time and blasted him with a final outburst.

CAW! CAW! CAW! CAW! CAW! CAW!

Greg felt something wet and heavy plop on his left shoulder. Even before he glanced at the green and white blob on his shirt, he knew what it was. "You gotta be kidding me!" He flicked the poop off his shoulder. "Stupid birds!" He looked at the disabled truck. "Stupid truck. Stupid vacation." Realizing his only option was to walk the two miles back to the landing, he stuffed his hands into his hip pockets and began walking, his shoulders drooped, biting his lip, and kicking at pebbles embedded in the sand. "Stupid sand."

He hadn't gone more than a few yards when he heard the distant rumbling of a car. Surprised, he looked up to see a swirling cloud of sandy smoke further down the road, coming toward him. "Thank God!" Just as he was beginning to feel excited about getting a ride, and feeling that everything would start going his way, the crows landed in a pine tree only a few yards away and resumed their harsh, obnoxious cawing. CAW! CAW! CAW! CAW!

Greg scooped up another handful of sand and whipped it at the feathered pests. "Get lost!"

The birds exploded from their perch and disappeared into the treetops.

Suddenly Greg became aware of the sound of a car engine idling behind him. From the corner of his eye, he saw a red convertible Mustang stopped in the road. His mouth fell open as he turned and stared at the driver, who was alone in the car.

Sitting behind the wheel was an attractive woman, 18 or 19 years old. She was wearing sunglasses and silver earrings, both of which glinted in the hot July sun. Her red hair was pulled back into a ponytail, with just a tuft of bangs hanging on her forehead. She cut the car's engine, then removed her sunglasses.

"What's up?" she asked, smiling. Matching dimples bordered her full red lips.

"Hi," Greg said, feeling a little shy. "My truck broke down. Could you give me a lift to town?"

"Sorry, kid ... I don't pick up strangers."

Greg's face clouded and he was about to object, but she beat him to it.

"Relax, kid ... I'm kidding!" she said, chuckling.

"Oh ... great," Greg said, forcing a smile. "You're a real riot."

"You got something against humor, kid? You look like you could use some right about now."

"Yeah, I guess I could at that." He walked up to the passenger side and leaned over the car, extending his hand. "I'm Greg. Greg Nelson."

"Lisa Barnett," she said, shaking his hand.

He noted how soft and feminine her hand felt. "What's that on your shoulder?" she asked.

Greg frowned. "Crow poop," he said, disgusted. "Darn birds got me good."

"Crow poop!" Lisa cried. "Uh, there's no way you're riding in *my* car with that crap on your shirt."

Greg stared at her incredulously, his mouth hanging open. "But, I—"

"Got you again, kid!" Lisa said, then leaned her head back and laughed.

"Very funny," Greg said, but not really seeing any humor in it. "I suppose it's funny as long as the crow bomb isn't smeared on *your* shirt."

"Crow bomb!" she cried, then erupted into laughter again, throwing her head back against the seat, covering her mouth with her hands. Gasping for air, she said, "Crow bomb! That's the funniest thing I ever heard." She broke into laughter again, tears rolling down her cheeks. Impulsively she pounded her steering wheel, tooting the car horn, making her laugh even harder.

That did it. It was too much for Greg to bear. Her laughter was too contagious to ignore. He finally broke down and laughed ... laughed hard. He couldn't stop. Soon, tears were rolling down *his* cheeks, as well. Leaning against the passenger door, he doubled over, holding his gut, laughing as he'd never laughed before.

Finally, Lisa caught her breath and wiped her eyes. "Whew! That was too much. You crack me up, kid." She smiled at him, her beautiful brown eyes still glistening with tears. "So what's up with your truck?"

Greg wiped his eyes and took a deep breath. "I don't kno—" He stopped abruptly as he watched her climb out of her car. She was dressed in a white halter top, blue jean short-shorts, and a pair of sandals. Her legs were long, smooth, and slender. Her tummy was flat and sexy. He couldn't help but notice that her bosom more than amply filled out her top. Suddenly he felt shy and nervous.

"Cat got your tongue?" she asked nonchalantly, poking her head under the hood. "Or should I say ... crow? Crow got your tongue?" She chuckled.

"Oh, God ... don't start that again," Greg said, standing behind her. He couldn't keep his eyes off her round bottom and bare legs. "I don't think I've ever laughed that hard in my life."

"Laughter's good for you. Releases dopamine and other good stuff into your system. It improves your immune system so you can fight off disease."

"I didn't know that," Greg said simply. He averted his eyes off her legs long enough to watch her unscrew the radiator cap and peer inside.

"Oh, sure ... it's a fact," she went on. "It even says so in your Bible: 'A cheerful heart is good medicine, but a crushed spirit dries up the bones.' Proverbs 17, verse 22."

"I didn't know that, either. Listen ... why don't you just give me a ride into town, and I'll have a tow truck come pick it up."

She remained bent over, tinkering under the hood. "You're not too bright, are you?" she said over her shoulder. "Anyone can see you're an out-of-towner. The mechanic will rip you off. So will the tow truck driver."

"But it's not even *my* truck. It belongs to Mr. Tucker ... you know ... from Tucker Island."

"Doesn't make any difference. They see you're from out of town, so they figure you got money—at least more money than they got. Anyhow, that's how they make a living ... by feeding off the tourists."

He folded his arms, watching her with skepticism. "So what are *you* going to do—fix my truck?" He snickered.

She pulled on some wiring, examined it. "Nope. I'm going to fix Mr. *Tucker's* truck. What's the matter, you don't believe a girl can fix cars?"

"I believe some girls *think* they can fix cars. I think they begin tinkering around with cars while they're still in high school just to impress their boyfriends. But let's face it. There's not too many girl mechanics around. I mean, how many girl mechanics do *you* see when *you* go to a garage for repairs?"

"I don't."

"Exactly!" Greg said, feeling in control now, putting this beautiful, but cocky girl in her place. "See what I mean?"

"I don't see any girl mechanics because I never go to a garage. And I never go to a garage because I do all my own car repairs." She looked over her shoulder at him and smiled.

"Yeah, well ... back home, I go to a garage all the time, and they don't have any girl mechanics working there."

She straightened up, shut the hood, and drew her arm across her brow. "Too bad for them. Shows how much *they* know. No wonder you have to keep going back to them for repairs." She smiled mischievously, her brown eyes flashing.

Greg let a little smile trickle across his lips. "I give up," he said, rolling his eyes.

Lisa removed a shop rag from the trunk of her car and wiped her hands on it. "Let me give you a little piece of advice, kid—never give up ... never."

Greg raised his eyebrows and sighed deeply.

"Anyhow, I'll drive you into town so you can pick up the parts you'll need to get your truck running."

"But I don't *know* what parts I need. That's why I'm gonna have it towed."

Lisa got in her car, slid her sunglasses back on, then started the motor. "In addition to a spare tire, you need a new fuel filter, radiator hose, and a thermostat." She smiled and patted the seat next to her. "Come on, kid ... get in."

On the way to town, Greg tried to explain to Lisa the events that had taken place yesterday on Mink Lake. But when he came to the part about the giant catfish, she stared at him intently, so disbelievingly, she almost steered the car off the road.

"Oh, great!" Greg cried. "That's all I need on top of everything else—a car accident. Look ... do you mind if *I* drive to the Wolverine town limits?"

Lisa punched the brakes with her foot, causing the Mustang to jerk to a stop amid a cloud of sandy dust.

Now *Greg* was staring in disbelief. "What'd you do that for?" he asked, waving dust away from his face.

Lisa snapped her head in his direction, glaring at him through dust-covered sunglasses, her lips pursed tightly into a knot. "Get out!"

The command caught Greg completely by surprise. "What!"

"You heard me! Get out!"

"What are you talking about? I thought you were giving me a ride into town."

Lisa tore the sunglasses off her face, glaring at him, her brown eyes ablaze with anger. "*That* was before you criticized my driving ... kid. Now get out!"

"Wait a minute! I wasn't criticizing your driving. I just didn't want you to wrap the car around a tree—that's all. You almost ran us off the road back there, you know."

"Ohhh ... wellll ... excuuuuuse *me*. Sometimes I do that when I got a jerk sitting beside me, telling me some stupid story about a giant catfish. I mean, first I find you wandering alone in the wilderness, throwing sand in the air, catching crow poop with your shirt, then I learn you know nothing about car repairs, and now you tell me a story about a giant catfish that gobbled up your dog. What are you ... some kind of *nut*case?"

Greg was fuming. After all he'd been through in the last

24 hours, and now *this?* Did he have the words, ABUSE ME, stamped on his forehead? *Nobody* deserved to be treated like this. Even his *sister* didn't deserve to be treated like *this*. "All right ... that's it. Get out!"

Lisa cocked her head at him, shocked. "What!"

Realizing his mistake, he said, "This is *your* car. *I'll* get out." He slammed the door shut behind him, feeling foolish and angry.

"Thank you," she said curtly, jamming the sunglasses back on her face.

"You're welcome," Greg replied sarcastically. "But I didn't make that story up. It really happened. And as soon as I get into Wolverine, I'm going straight to Sheriff Clifford's office to file a report."

"How nice for you," she said, then floored the gas pedal, leaving him behind in a cloud of sandy dust.

Greg watched the Mustang, engulfed in the dust cloud, disappear around a bend. In less than a minute, there was nothing to see but a ribbon of sand, winding between two walls of evergreens that reached into a bright blue sky. *Stupid broad,* he thought, scratching his head. *I can't believe this.*

Up ahead, an entire flock of crows glided above the road, swooping and diving, their loud, harsh cawing shattering the early morning tranquility of the surrounding forest. Some of them landed on the shoulder of the road, perhaps to scavenge a roadside deer carcass that might be lying in the weeds.

Greg eyed them with contempt. He spotted a large, heavy stick lying on the shoulder of the road. He snatched it up and began walking toward town, heading straight for the crows. "Beat it!" he yelled, waving the stick. He was still some distance from the flock when he heard the distant rumbling of a car again. *No, it can't be. No way. She's gone for good.*

His mouth fell open when a mini dust storm swirled around the bend into view, heading toward him. As it drew closer, he could see a splash of red inside the dust cloud. "Well, I'll be ..." Moments later, the Mustang passed him, slowed, made a U-turn, then crept up alongside of him and stopped.

Lisa's face showed complete disinterest, but the fact that she had returned belied her feigned apathy. "So what's the stick for?" she asked nonchalantly.

Blushing, Greg immediately threw it down, wiped his hands on his jeans. "Nothing."

"Uh-huh. I thought maybe a tyrannosaurus rex hopped out of the woods and started chasing you or something."

Greg bit his lip, his face still dark with color. "You're back."

"Come on, kid. Get in. And tell me some more about that giant catfish."

"I thought you didn't believe me," he said, sliding into the seat beside her.

"I don't, but I just have to see Sheriff Clifford's face when you tell *him* your story." She put the car in gear and headed for town.

The town of Wolverine had a population of only 800 people. A good many of the residents were retired folks. Most of them had been store clerks, farmers, hired hands, teachers, loggers, and railroad workers. Many of them had had to earn a meager living in the larger neighboring town of Pine Acres, population 35,000, which was situated some 60 miles to the north of Wolverine. A couple of dozen Wolverine residents had been lucky enough to land jobs at the nuclear power plant located between Wolverine and Pine Acres just off of State Highway 43, which ran north and south through the hearts of both towns. But of course, their jobs vanished when the plant had been closed down after only a few years of operation, leaving most of them still unemployed.

The actual town of Wolverine was nothing more than a stretch of Highway 43 about a mile long, bordered on both sides by a string of various shops and stores: a post office, barber shop, beauty salon, bakery shop, taxidermy shop, gunsmith, clothing store, hardware store, drugstore, three bait and tackle shops, two motels, three cafes, three gas stations, a grade school, a high school, a lumber yard, two churches, four taverns, a fire station, and Sheriff Clifford's office and jail. Any goods or services not available in Wolverine would have to be obtained 60 miles away in Pine Acres. The closest town to the south of Wolverine was Woodstream, 100 miles away.

Meandering through town in a giant "S" shape was the Wolverine River, which intersected the highway in three different locations, forming a giant dollar ($) sign. Thus, the only way in or out of Wolverine was via Highway 43, and one had to cross three different bridges in order to pass completely through town: one on the north end, one in the middle of town, and one on the south end.

Because Mink Lake was located ten miles to the south of Wolverine, Greg and Lisa approached the town limits from the southern end, driving over an old plank bridge to cross the Wolverine River.

During the drive to town, Greg had learned that Lisa was spending the summer all alone at her parents' cabin on Mink Lake. She told him that her parents were in the midst of a nasty divorce, that she was an only child, she had graduated from high school last year, she was 18 years old, still living at home, but needed to get away by herself for a few months because of the intense friction and turmoil at home brought on by the divorce.

Greg couldn't imagine what it would be like to have parents constantly screaming at each other, threatening one another, because Mom and Dad got along fabulously well—most of the time. Oh, sure, he bickered almost nonstop with Jenny—the little brat—who wouldn't? And Dad never missed an opportunity to rag on him, needle him, criticize him, make him feel inadequate. But no matter how bitchy things got at home, he always felt that he had a home, a rock-solid place where he could always depend on Mom and Dad sticking together and being there for him if he ever needed them. The more he thought about it, the more he realized that home wasn't such a bad place after all. But just think of how much better it would be if Jenny weren't there! Too harsh, he thought. She's not *that* bad. I'd settle for her not being able to speak. That would work!

"I'm sorry about your parents," he said sincerely, as they rolled into town.

Lisa glanced at him, surprised. Parking the Mustang in front of the sheriff's office, she cut the engine, then sat and stared at him. "So what are you doing for supper tonight?"

Greg was taken aback by the question. Was it an invitation? If so, it was the first time any girl had ever asked *him* for a date. Even though he was six-feet-tall, lean, tan, and muscular, back home he wasn't exactly known as "Mr. Popularity" around the girls. If he had any hope of ever going on a date, it was always up to him to do the asking. And even then his success rate was only 50% at best. Why only half the girls asked would ever accept, he didn't know. Last year Marianne Becker—one of the girls he had dated—had told him he was "emotionally immature." That hurt. Of course it was a lot of nonsense. She probably had said that because he had told her that he liked to "mess around" with remote control toys. Once he had suggested that they go to the park to fly one of his remote control airplanes. So what was wrong with that? Anyway, what else could have made her say that about him? After all, he was a pretty cool dude, what with his scuba diving, karate, dirt bike racing, and pistol target practice—with a .357 magnum, no less. You couldn't get more macho than that. Nevertheless, the remark had gnawed at him for a long time afterward, undermining his self-confidence. He frowned, chewing on his lower lip. The heck with Marianne Becker. "What'd ya have in mind?"

"Ohhh, I thought maybe we could have a weenie roast around a campfire at my place tonight."

"Sounds good. I'll be there, but first I'll have to stop back at my cabin and pick up some clothes and things for me, Jenny, and the twins. We left in such a hurry for Tucker Island yesterday, we didn't have time to pack anything. How about eight o'clock?"

Her smile was warm and radiant. "Fine. On the way home from town, I'll show you where I live so you can find it later tonight."

The two of them got out of the car and climbed a couple of steps onto the veranda that was attached to the front of the building. The veranda was constructed of thick posts and heavy beams that supported a wooden plank roof. The floor was also made of wooden planks that had been worn smooth from years of sandy grit being ground into the rough boards from heavy foot traffic. The main structure was brick, but the front of the building had been built of large, irregular-shaped field stones. The front door was vertical oak planks bolted together with strap iron, and hung in place with iron strap hinges. A twelve inch square hole had been cut into the door about five and a half feet up from the bottom to serve as a window. Though the window had glass in it, thick iron bars crisscrossed the opening in front of the glass. The large picture windows on either side of the door were also barricaded with iron bars.

"Looks like something out of an old John Wayne movie," Greg said, awestruck by the formidable structure.

"Yeah, well, I can assure you that the sheriff is nothing at all like John Wayne."

"What do you mean?"

Lisa grabbed the iron door latch, hesitated, and looked at Greg. The slightest trace of apprehension showed on her face. "You'll see." She pushed the heavy door open and walked in.

Greg followed reluctantly, aware of his nerve suddenly slipping away.

Inside was a large, dark room that reeked of cigar smoke. The walls were covered with wood paneling that gave way to a high, plastered ceiling. Suspended from the dirty-white ceiling was a large ceiling fan, spinning at what appeared to be full-speed. The wood-grain blades whirred softly, slicing effortlessly through the hot, stale air.

The dirty, gray-black concrete floor was littered with gum wrappers, paper clips, rubber bands, and cigar butts—short, shredded, spongy-looking, chewed-up, brown, slimy cigar butts. In a corner of the room sat a large, ancient oak desk, littered with papers and files. Jutting from the desktop debris was a round glass ashtray, heaping with more of the brown, slimy butts. Next to the ashtray was a black telephone, glistening with dirty palm grease. On the wall behind the desk, a door stood ajar, revealing a toilet so old and primitive-looking, Greg guessed it had been installed before the ice age. He grimaced at the yellow and orange-brown rivers of pee stains that had dried on the outside of the bowl. He prayed he wouldn't have to use the restroom during his visit. No telling *what* you could catch from *that* toilet seat.

A wooden gun rack hung on the wall next to the restroom door. It was loaded with at least two dozen rifles and shotguns of various calibers and gauges. Greg noted the arsenal was every bit as impressive as Mr. Tucker's—except for the lack of an AK-47 assault rifle. Even a sheriff doesn't need one of those, he reasoned. This isn't exactly New York City or Los Angeles. Not that *they* would use AK-47's for police work. But they are big cities, and big cities have SWAT teams, and SWAT teams do use automatic weapons of one kind or another. He grinned inside, imagining a small, resort town sheriff pulling out an AK-47 to arrest some poor farmer for drunk driving or fishing without a license or littering the back roads with empty beer cans. Ridiculous.

Along the wall opposite the gun rack was a row of metal, four-drawer, army-tank-green file cabinets. There must have been a dozen of them, all lined up straight, but dented, dusty, and scratched, like a row of shabby soldiers standing at attention. The dented and dusty tops of the cabinets served as a catchall for a vast array of office supplies and miscellaneous junk, including dozens of empty cigar boxes.

Six wooden chairs lined the wall next to the front door. Greg guessed that the large, battered chairs were at least as old as the dinosaur desk. On the wall directly opposite the chairs was an oak door that was partially open. Beyond the door was a long corridor with a concrete floor, harshly illuminated by a string of bare light bulbs hanging from the ceiling. Black iron bars, stretching from the floor to the ceiling, lined the hallway on both sides. At the end of the corridor was another heavy wooden door with a thick iron bar lying across its width, resting in iron brackets on either side of the door.

Greg heard voices coming from the rear of the corridor. It sounded as if someone were shouting. The other voice was crying, pleading, as though someone were in pain and was begging for it to stop. Greg felt his stomach turn over, and sat down. He motioned for Lisa to sit down. She plunked herself in a chair next to him, crossing her long, slender legs. She sighed, indicating boredom.

The flat, dead sound of someone being punched erupted from the rear of the corridor. A cry of pain immediately followed.

Greg looked at Lisa, frowning, alarm in his eyes. "What's going on back there?"

Lisa removed a nail file from her purse, and began to file her nails. "That's just Sheriff Clifford doing what he does best—hurting people," she said casually.

Greg stared at her incredulously. "What!"

More punching sounds.

More screaming.

Greg sprung from his chair. "Maybe we should come back later."

"Relax, kid. He's got no beef with you. Come on ... sit down."

At the sound of a steel cell door clanging shut, Greg peered down the hall and swallowed hard when he saw a very large man, with a silver badge pinned on his shirt, swagger down the corridor toward him. He was staring at Greg, staring at him through double-thick glasses, his eyes cold and piercing.

The man wasn't big. He was *huge*—at least six-and-a-half-feet tall, three hundred and fifty pounds. He stood in the doorway, grinning, staring at Lisa's legs. He was wearing rubber gloves, the kind doctors and dentists use—thin, white latex gloves. Only his gloves weren't completely white—they were splattered with blood. "Hello, Lisa. Long time no see." His voice was deep and gruff. "How's your mother?"

Lisa shot him a glance, then resumed her nail filing. "Hello, Sheriff Clifford. I see you're busy as usual—beating up another prisoner."

Greg stared in shocked silence as the huge man moved across the room, stripped off his gloves, and dropped them into a gray metal wastebasket beside the desk.

"First time I've seen you since last summer, and already you're starting with your smart mouth." He let himself plop into a large wooden swivel chair behind his desk, clasped his hands behind his head, and propped his enormous feet up on the desktop, spilling papers onto the floor. "Is this going to be a long summer, Lisa?"

"Beats me," she replied, never taking her eyes off her nails.

"Who's your friend?"

Greg felt his stomach turn over again. His palms grew sweaty. His heartbeat quickened. He thought of excusing himself and walking out the front door, right then and there. After all, he didn't *have* to stay and talk to the sheriff. And who cared what Lisa would think of him. He just met her, for crying out loud. Obviously she knew the sheriff, was familiar with his ways, his rude sarcastic manner. And obviously she was prepared to put up with it. But he wasn't. He didn't come all the way here to take any crap from anyone. He was about to reach for the door, then stopped, remembering what Marianne Becker had called him: emotionally immature. And then he remembered why he had come here in the first place: to tell the sheriff what had happened to Spook, and what had almost happened to little Timmy. He pushed past his fear, and forced himself to face the gross, sadistic hulk. He walked up to the sheriff's desk and stuck out his hand.

"Hi, Sheriff. I'm Greg Nelson from Mink Lake." He managed a weak smile.

Sheriff Clifford was wearing construction-type, leather work boots. He let them drop to the floor, sat up in his chair, reached into a drawer, and withdrew a cigar. He struck a wooden match on his desktop, then cupped the match and the cigar in his beefy hands. He threw the match on the floor, then blew a thin stream of gray smoke out of his mouth. The room quickly filled with the acrid smell, and soon the gray smoke was swirling about the sheriff's head. He leaned back in his chair, placed his feet back on the desktop, and re-clasped his hands behind his head, the long brown cigar jutting from his massive jaw. "So?"

Greg withdrew his hand, letting it drop to his side, aware of his smile waning. He was also aware of his palms growing more and more sweaty—both from nervousness *and* from anger. Cool it! he thought, keeping eye contact with the sheriff. I'm not going to let this fat, rude slob get the better of me. Who does he think he is, anyway? He shot an inquisitive look at Lisa, who looked up at him, raised her eyebrows, and shrugged. He turned to the sheriff, cleared his throat, and began relating his story about the giant catfish and Spook and the attack on Timmy.

All the while Greg spoke, Sheriff Clifford sat staring at Lisa's legs, puffing profusely on his cigar, letting the ashes drop on his inflated belly. Little piles of gray-black ashes began to accumulate on the yards of beige material that made up the top portion of his uniform.

When Greg had finished telling his story, the sheriff flicked the cigar from his mouth. It landed on the concrete floor with a soft ...PLOP! Then he placed his cantaloupe hands on his heaving chest, and glared at Greg, his thick, black brows lowered into a continuous bristling band. "Did you tell this story to anyone else?" His tone was serious—deadly serious.

Greg felt himself cringing. Suddenly he wished he hadn't come to the sheriff after all. "Just Lisa and the Tuckers," he replied, a trace of stress in his voice. The stuffy room was growing hotter by the minute. He wiped his palms on his jeans.

Sheriff Clifford rose slowly from his chair, never removing his eyes from Greg. He came around to the front of the desk and stood before Greg, looming over him. "What'd you say your name was?"

"Greg." His voice squeaked out. He cleared his throat. "Greg Nelson."

"Well, Mr. Greg Nelson ... I think we have a problem here."

Greg felt relieved. At last someone would believe him. Someone with authority. Someone who could do something about it. Someone who *would* do something about it. Now he was glad—darn glad—he had come to the sheriff.

Sheriff Clifford placed his hands on his hips, his face bearing down into Greg's. "You ever do drugs, son?"

The question took Greg completely by surprise. Suddenly his stomach fluttered, and he felt a sickening wave of doom wash over him. "What!"

The sheriff's gaze never wavered. His cold, piercing eyes seemed to knife through Greg's eyes and plunge into his soul, laying it bare for all the world to see. "You heard me ... drugs. You taking drugs, son?"

"No, of course not!"

Sheriff Clifford's eyes widened, as if he were taken aback by the negative response. "No, of course not!" he scoffed, then laughed harshly. "No, of course not! No, of course not!" He laughed some more, loud and gruff. "Maybe you'd have a different answer if I took you in the back room and asked you. Shall I get another pair of gloves?"

Lisa jammed her nail file in her purse, and sprang from her chair. "He's not one of your prisoners, Sheriff!" she snapped.

Sheriff Clifford spun around, leveling a sausage finger at her. "That'll be enough of *your* mouth, little lady," he roared.

Lisa's face was strained and dark with color. To Greg she said, "Let's go, kid. You told him your story ... now it's time to leave." She headed for the front door, and Greg quickly followed, bewildered and resentful.

"Just remember this," Sheriff Clifford called after them, "you two go around town telling folks that cock and bull story about a giant catfish, and I promise you—I'll arrest you, I'll throw you in my jail, and then you *will* be my prisoners."

Just outside the closed door, Greg scolded Lisa. "What'd you do that for?"

Lisa snapped her head toward him, shocked. "What!"

"You jump in and defend me, and then you haul me out of there like I was your little boy or something."

Lisa's eyes were as big as saucers, as she stared at him, completely flabbergasted. "What!"

"I can handle myself, you know. I don't need you or anyone else coming to my rescue. And I don't need you telling me what to do, ordering me around like I was a child." Greg felt his face grow hot. It was flushed with fury.

She shook her head, astonished, her mouth grasping for words. "I don't believe this kid! Do you always act this irrational?"

"And don't call me kid anymore. I'm not your kid! And I don't like you calling me kid. It's annoying. So knock it off. Understand?" His heart was pounding. A part of him was glad to have told her off, let her know how he felt. But another side of him wasn't so sure he had done the right thing. For he suddenly realized he had no problem showing his anger and standing up to Jenny or Lisa, but when it came to telling off Dad or Sheriff Clifford—that was another story. What kind of man am I? he wondered, suddenly regretting his outburst.

Lisa pursed her lips, her eyes wide with anger. "You jerk! I just saved your butt in there!" She grabbed a fistful of his T-shirt, hitting him in the chest, startling him, catching him completely off guard. "So you're a big man, huh?" she yelled, her lips drawn back, revealing her teeth like a rabid dog. "You can handle yourself, huh?" She reached for the door latch with her free hand, and opened the door. Then, while shoving him inside, she said, "Why don't you go and tell the sheriff what a big man you are?" Then she spun around and marched to her car, leaving Greg standing there, shocked and bewildered.

Sheriff Clifford was in the process of lighting another cigar. He looked up at Greg, stunned. "What the hell do you want?"

Embarrassed, Greg straightened his T-shirt and ran a hand over his flattop. He was speechless. "Uh … sorry, Your Honor. I mean, Chief. I mean, Sheriff. Have a nice day." He scrambled outside, closing the door behind him. "Damn!"

Lisa had backed the Mustang out of the parking space and was just about to drive off when he stopped her. He ran in front of the car, waving his arms. "Lisa, wait!"

She was wearing her sunglasses again, and her lips were still pursed.

God, she looks mad, he thought, walking around to the driver's side. "I'm sorry, Lisa. I shouldn't have said those things. I was out of line. I'm sorry—I really am."

The car was in "DRIVE," engine idling, but she had her foot on the brake so the car wouldn't move. She stared straight ahead through her dark shades.

"Look, Greg ... it was nice meeting you and everything, but I have things to do now, and you have things to do now. So it's time to say goodbye. So goodbye and good luck." She started to drive away.

"Lisa, wait!" Greg shouted. "Will you just wait a minute!"

She stopped. "Now what?"

"Look ... I said I was sorry, and I meant it. I shouldn't have ragged on you like that. It's just that I felt ... inadequate and helpless in there. I mean ...my little brother was almost killed yesterday, for crying out loud. And I can't even get anybody to believe me. Everybody just wants to give me an argument about it—including you. Why don't you just come with me to Tucker Island and talk to Jenny and the twins. They were there. They saw it. They'll tell ya."

Silence, except for the sound of the running motor.

"Get in, Greg. We got work to do."

He looked at her, confused. He opened the door and slid in beside her. "Where to?"

"Well, first we'll go to the garage and buy the parts for your truck."

"Mr. Tucker's truck," he reminded her. "And I don't have any money." Sitting beside her, he could see behind her sunglasses from the side angle. She was rolling her eyes.

"Okay, okay ... it's Mr. Tucker's truck, and I'll loan you the money. We'll put it on my credit card. After the garage, we'll go to the grocery store, which is where I was headed when I met you. Then we'll drive back to the truck, I'll repair it, and then we'll stop by my place to unload the groceries."

Greg's pulse quickened at the words, "my place." He had never been in a situation before where he had been home all alone with a beautiful girl at *her* place. "What do we do after we put the groceries away?"

She grinned. "Not what you're thinking. We're going to take my speedboat out and take a look around the lake. See if we can find anything. Maybe talk to some of the locals."

"You believe me, then?" he asked hopefully.

"I didn't say that." She swung the car into a Shell station lot and parked it. With a flick of her finger, she knocked her sunglasses down on her nose and peered over them. "I believe you guys saw *something* out there yesterday ... but a giant catfish? You have to admit ...it's hard to believe." Greg started to protest, but she cut him off. "Come on, let's go shopping for some truck parts."

Later that morning, after shopping in town, they returned to Mr. Tucker's truck. Greg helped her change the flat with a spare tire loaned to them by a mechanic named Gus at the Shell station. Now Greg watched her as she slipped into a denim coverall she had fetched from the Mustang's trunk, along with a red metal toolbox. Somehow seeing her inside her grease-stained suit, the tip of her flaming red ponytail poking at the coverall's tattered collar, her flashy silver earrings bouncing against her smooth, unblemished face, a wrench clutched in her soft, white hand with polished nails, he found her extremely beautiful, dazzling, radiant.

He was surprised at his attraction to her, for at first he had felt jealousy and resentment toward her because of her brash, bold behavior, and—he admitted to himself—because of her mechanical skills. He grinned now, recalling how, inside the Shell station, she had embarrassed him by announcing to all of the mechanics on duty that *she* was buying parts for *his* truck so that *she* could go and repair it for *him*. The mechanics, who obviously knew her on a first-name basis, had laughed and joked with her, teasing her good-naturedly. They had barely even looked at Greg, let alone talked to him. He couldn't help but notice that every eye in the place had been on Lisa—every man lavishing her with attention and obvious affection.

But that hadn't been the worst of it. After the Shell station, they had gone shopping at Wally's Finer Foods, just down the street. At the checkout counter, Greg had felt foolish as Lisa once again whipped out her wallet and paid for the groceries. Sure, they were *her* groceries, but he had felt like a little boy whose mommy had taken him shopping, nevertheless. But the worst part came when a box of tampons, riding alongside the hot dogs and buns, had glided past him on the conveyor. He had glanced at Lisa, embarrassed.

Lisa had made no attempt to keep her voice low. "What's the matter—haven't you ever seen tampons before?"

The pretty blond cashier had glanced up at him and smiled. Greg had felt like crawling under the counter to hide his hot, flaming face. It had been a most unpleasant and embarrassing experience, and he had resented her for it.

But now as he watched her working under the hood of the truck, dirtying her hands, a smudge of black grease on her chin, her blue denim bottom jutting out from under the green metal canopy, his jealousy and resentment were slowly but most assuredly, turning into a deep, profound fondness for her.

Later, after the truck was repaired, Greg followed Lisa to her cabin and helped her put the groceries away. Then Greg drove both of them in Mr. Tucker's truck to Greg's cabin to pick up clothes and supplies for himself, Jenny, and the twins. Greg and Lisa loaded everything into Mr. Tucker's speedboat, then Lisa followed Greg in her speedboat to Tucker Island, where they unloaded the supplies and carried them into the house. After all the introductions had been made, Greg and Lisa left in Lisa's speedboat to cruise the lake, looking for fishermen whom they could interview, searching for any clues or information that would lead to the discovery of the giant catfish.

Later, their investigative expedition was turning out to be a bust. After talking to half a dozen fishermen, they were getting nowhere. None of them had seen or heard of anything unusual on the lake. Some of them were indignant and resented Greg and Lisa for invading the fishing space around their boats.

"Thank God we didn't come right out and ask them if they had seen a giant catfish," Lisa said, steering her speedboat back to Tucker Island. Greg would get Mr. *Tucker's* speedboat, then follow Lisa back to her cabin, where they would have dinner together.

"I just don't get it," Greg shouted above the roar of the motor. "I know it's a big lake, but—" Something caught his attention from the corner of his eye. He snapped his head to the right, just in time to see an enormous underwater shadow, gliding just beneath the surface like a 15- or 20-foot torpedo. It was heading straight toward a loon swimming on the surface. "LISA LOOK!" he yelled, pointing frantically.

Lisa instantly killed the engine and scrambled beside Greg. Clutching the boat's railing with one hand, and shading her eyes with the other, she leaned over the side, straining, searching the water. "I don't see anything. Just a loon."

"But it was just there! I swear! I just saw it!" But whatever Greg had seen, it was now gone. "Where'd it go!"

Lisa shrugged and returned to the steering wheel. "I'm getting hungry," she said, starting the boat's motor. "How about that weenie roast?"

Still staring at the water, his face scrunched, Greg shook his head. "I just don't get it," he said, perplexed. "I could've sworn I saw it."

Lisa opened the throttle, and they zipped across Mink Lake toward Tucker Island. All the while, Greg kept his gaze on the loon, expecting it to disappear any second. But the loon remained undisturbed.

Later that evening, Greg and Lisa sat under a full moon around a campfire on the beach at Lisa's cabin. They roasted hot dogs and marshmallows on long, slender birch twigs held above the flicking flames, and drank Diet Pepsi's.

The moon's silvery reflection glittered on the lake's calm surface. Somewhere far beyond the reflection, a loon called out in the darkness. Its mournful and maniacal cry fluctuated from a slow, guttural note to a fast, frenzied pitch. A feathery breeze whispered through the forest, carrying with it the pleasant scent of pine. The air was warm and dry.

Along the shoreline, hidden in the darkness, bullfrogs everywhere bellowed their deep, aching chorus: RRRRRRRIBBIT! RRRRRRRIBBIT! RRRRRRRIBBIT!

In the surrounding forest, crickets answered the croaky music with a soft, chirpy melody of their own.

"Sure is a nice night," Greg said, gazing up at the brilliant stars sparkling in the night sky. He popped the last bite of his hot dog into his mouth, then washed it down with a swig of soda.

"Yes it is," Lisa agreed, staring heavenward. She drew her knees up to her chest and wrapped her arms around her bare legs. "It's so balmy and peaceful. So ... romantic."

Greg scooted over, sitting next to her in the sand. He let his gaze fall upon her face, expecting to find her watching the stars. But instead, she was watching *him,* staring dreamily, expectantly at him, her lips full and sensuous in the glow of firelight. His heart fluttered, as he leaned in and kissed her.

She wrapped her arms around him and kissed him back—

with passion. Afterward, she looked into his eyes and smiled warmly, then turned her gaze to the campfire, resting her head against his shoulder. "That was nice."

Greg sat with his arm around her, holding her close. "Yeah … it was." He felt ashamed of himself for having harbored any petty, negative feelings earlier toward this warm, beautiful girl with the wonderful sense of humor. Time to grow up, he thought. "It's getting late … I'd better be going. Got a big day tomorrow. I'm gonna find that monster if it's the last thing I do." He stood up, then reached down and helped Lisa to her feet. "Thanks for everything. I really appreciate it."

"You're welcome. I'm glad I was able to help."

He kissed her, then started walking toward the pier where Mr. Tucker's speedboat was docked.

"Well, wait a minute!" she called, running after him.

He stopped on the pier and waited for her.

Her face was softly illuminated by moonlight. "I'll go with you tomorrow."

"You may not want to," Greg said. "Tomorrow I'm gonna go around the whole lake and ask everyone and anyone— right out—if they've ever seen that catfish in this lake. I'm not fooling around anymore—I'm getting to the bottom of this, once and for all! Somebody's got to know something."

Her silver earrings shimmered in the moonlight. "Aren't you forgetting what Sheriff Clifford said he'd do if he found out you were spreading your story around about a giant catfish?" she asked.

"I'm not worried about that stupid sheriff." He turned and looked out at the lake, into the darkness. "There's a monster out there, Lisa. And I'm going to find it."

"Yeah, sure. If Sheriff Clifford doesn't find you first." Lisa shivered and folded her arms across her chest. "You don't know Sheriff Clifford like I do, Greg."

Greg started to climb into Mr. Tucker's boat, then stopped, looked up at her. "How *do* you know Sheriff Clifford?"

"He used to come around and hit on my mother whenever she came up here without my dad."

Greg wrinkled his nose. "Hit on her?"

"Yeah, you know ... come on to her, asking her for a date, stuff like that."

"Does that have anything to do with your parents' divorce?"

"Oh, God, no. My dad never knew that Sheriff Clifford had the hots for my mom. And besides, my mom would *never* have anything to do with that creep. Basically, she always told him to get lost or drop dead. But he's weird, you know? It seemed like the more Mom told him to buzz off, the more aggressive and turned on he would get. The guy's a freak. And he's got a real problem taking 'no' for an answer." She shuddered. "He gives me the willies."

Greg recalled the way Sheriff Clifford had been staring at—practically drooling over—Lisa's legs earlier that morning in town. He told her about it.

"Oh, my God! Now I won't be able to sleep tonight."

Greg was puzzled. "Why not?"

"Well, you never know ...he may come knocking on *my* door." She grabbed both his hands and gazed into his eyes. "Would you mind if I came with you and spent the night at Tucker Island? I promise not to be a bother. And we can get an early start tomorrow, cruising the lake, talking to fishermen."

She's so beautiful, so vulnerable, he thought, his eyes searching her face. All day long she makes out like she's cool and tough, but I think she's scared. Really scared. "Well, I don't know," he teased. "How will that look to the Tuckers when I come home with a beautiful girl, and ask them if she can spend the night?"

Her sparkling brown eyes were pleading with him, begging him. "Please?" Her voice was soft, seductive. Her smooth, white face glowed softly in the pillowy moonlight.

Greg stepped down inside Mr. Tucker's speedboat. He loosened the ropes that kept the craft tied to the pier, then sat in the driver's seat, preparing to start the outboard motor.

"Well?" she asked, frowning, her hands on her hips.

He turned the key in the ignition, and the motor roared alive. He looked up at her and smiled. "Coming?"

Suddenly she exploded with enthusiasm. "I'll be right back!" she cried, running toward the cabin. "I need a change of clothes and a toothbrush! Don't you dare leave without me, Greg Nelson!"

Later, after crossing the lake under the full moon, Greg edged the boat alongside the Tuckers' dock. His eye caught a metal chain fish stringer hanging from the end of the pier, glinting in the moonlight. The end of the stringer was submerged in the lake. Cutting the motor, he pointed to the stringer and said, "Looks like Mr. Tucker took the twins fishing today. Let's see what they caught." He grabbed a four-cell flashlight from the storage box between the two front seats, then helped Lisa out of the boat. After securing the boat to the dock, he switched on the flashlight, took Lisa's hand, then strolled to the end of the pier.

Lisa responded to the handholding gesture by leaning her head on his shoulder. "You know, in all the years we've been coming up here, I've never gone fishing."

"What!" Greg said, surprised. "You gotta be kidding!" He couldn't imagine anyone coming up here to this beautiful country—God's country—and not do a little fishing. "You've been missing a lot of fun. We'll have to take care of that." He knelt down at the edge of the pier and lifted the stringer out of the water. "Now, let's see what we got here," he said, shining his flashlight over the edge of the pier.

Lisa leaned over beside him, her hand on his shoulder. He sensed that her anticipation was as great as his own.

Glistening in the beam of light, on the end of the stringer, were six very large largemouth bass, the smallest of which must've weighed at least five pounds.

"Holy cow!" Greg cried, struggling with one hand against the weight of the fish. "I've never seen anything like this! These bass are *huge!* I can't believe—"

An explosion erupted in the dusky water in front of him, and he heard Lisa scream. The black, glistening head of the giant catfish rocketed out of the water, and its four-foot-wide mouth clamped shut around the stringer of fish, biting through the chain just beneath Greg's hand. "Jesus!"

Instantly the creature slid beneath the murky surface, back into the darkness. A millisecond later, the giant sprang from the lake again, its gigantic head smashing into the pier, its massive mouth missing Greg and Lisa by a fraction of an inch.

The pier shuddered, then collapsed under the tremendous force, and the last thing Greg heard before falling into the lake was Lisa's screams, then the sound of her body hitting the water.

CHAPTER 5

Her screaming shattered the stillness of the night, echoing above the lake's flat surface. "GREG! HELP ME! OH, MY GOD! GREEEEEEEEEEEEG!"

Greg's heart hammered in his chest, blood pounding inside his temples. Still clutching the flashlight, he trained the beam of light in the direction of Lisa's screams. He saw her thrashing in the water on the other side of the pier, only ten feet away. "Lisa! Hang on! I'm over here! Hang on! I'm coming!" He ducked beneath the pier and emerged on the same side as her. Though the water was only five feet deep, she whipped her arms around his neck and clung to him the way a person might do if they had just been rescued from drowning. "It's okay," he said, wrapping his arm around her waist. "I've got you."

But suddenly she screamed in his ear, pointing at the water a few feet away.

He jerked his head around in time to see the enormous creature, illuminated in the edge of the flashlight's ray, gliding directly at them like an underwater guided missile. There was no time to lose, no time to think. He shoved Lisa between two thick posts supporting the midsection of pier, then slipped through the opening himself. Trapped beneath the pier, he felt the giant slam into the posts behind him. The water swelled and rushed around him, heaving him up so high that his head bumped the underside of the pier's deck. Instinctively he spun around, flashlight in hand, ready to defend himself. He hunched beneath the pier, behind the safety of the posts, standing face to face with the deadly monster. Its black, beady eyes were cold and sinister, its gaze caught in the light beam, staring through Greg like a demon from hell. Its long, fleshy barbels floated and swirled in the water, resembling gigantic cat whiskers. The tip of one brushed against Greg's face, causing him to screech and jerk back impulsively.

In a flash the monster was gone.

"Let's get out of here!" Greg cried, reaching for Lisa's hand.

But the beast suddenly reappeared, bulldozing its massive head into the posts.

Greg could hear boards cracking and splintering overhead.

The monster rammed the posts again and again. The pier creaked and moaned.

Behind him, Greg felt Lisa clinging to him, glued to his back. She was screaming.

The monster veered away, then returned again, slamming into the posts like an underwater locomotive. The posts tore loose from the overhead beam with a tremendous wrenching noise. Greg felt the sandy bottom beneath him shudder from the blow. The posts were now spread three feet wider apart. One more blast from the charging giant would surely uproot the posts completely, leaving Greg and Lisa helpless before the predator.

As the creature whipped away from them again, readying itself for another attack, Greg grabbed Lisa's hand. "It's now or never!" he cried, and led her out between the posts supporting the other side of the pier—the side furthest from the monster. "Let's go!"

He scrambled on top of the deck, then helped pull up Lisa. Holding hands, they raced along the length of dock and stepped safely on shore just as the midsection of pier collapsed.

* * *

Later, inside the Tuckers' living room, after changing into dry clothes, Greg sat on the sofa with Timmy and Tommy tucked under each arm. Lisa was upstairs changing into some of Jenny's clothes. Lisa's clothes were still inside her overnight bag, which was now at the bottom of the lake. She had been holding the bag at the time she had fallen off the pier.

Mrs. Tucker was in the kitchen, fetching sodas for everyone.

Mr. Tucker had gone outside to observe the damage done to his pier. He had only raised an eyebrow when Greg had explained to him what had happened. Then he had quietly risen from his rocking chair, reached up on the mantel above the fireplace and took down an old kerosene lantern. After lighting it, he had strolled silently out the front door with it, his pipe jutting from his mouth, pipe smoke trailing behind him.

Timmy looked up at Greg, his eyes wide with excitement. "Gweg, did you weally see the monn-stor again?"

Greg's heartbeat was just now returning to normal. "You bet I did, Timmy." He envisioned the black, beady eyes from hell, and a shiver tingled up and down his spine. "But it's not really a monster, you know. It's only a catfish—a giant catfish." A giant *man-eating* catfish, he thought. Jeeez! What are we going to do?

Tommy burst open with a question of his own. "Is it going to get us, Gweg?" His small, freckled face was clouded, strained.

"No, of course not," Greg answered, then rubbed his hand over Tommy's fuzzy haircut. "I won't let anything happen to you guys. I ... I love you guys." He thought about that last statement, suddenly realizing he'd never said *that* before. And then it dawned on him—he felt the same way about Jenny. Even though he had never said it, when it came right down to it, he loved his annoying, bratty, little sister, too. Jeez, what's next?

Tommy looked up at him with worried eyes, his lower lip protruding, almost quivering. "Pwomise?"

"I promise. And I want you guys to promise me something, too."

The twins looked at him inquisitively, eyes blinking.

"I want you guys to promise me that you won't go fishing with Mr. Tucker again until we catch this giant catfish. Promise me you won't go anywhere *near* the lake. Okay?"

"Okay," they chimed. "We pwomise."

"Gweg?" Timmy asked.

"Yeah?"

"How you gonna catch it?"

"You can use my fishing pole!" Tommy cried. "It's stwong, 'cause I caught a big bass with it today!"

"I don't think we can catch it with a fishing pole," Greg said, eyeing the gun cabinet in the corner. "We're going to need something a lot more powerful than a fishing rod."

Mrs. Tucker scurried into the room, carrying a trayful of sodas. "Okay, there's Coke and Seven-up for everyone." She placed the tray on the knotty pine coffee table. "Help yourselves. I'll be right back with some pretzels."

Greg watched her with amusement as she bustled toward the kitchen again. *Lisa and I were almost killed tonight, and she's throwing a party!* he thought. *It's like she can't grasp the idea that there's real danger out there. She can't—or won't—face the reality of it. She acts like she doesn't want to hear about it or talk about it. Weird!*

Mr. Tucker came in the front door, frowning. He extinguished the lantern by blowing out the flame, then replaced it on top of the mantel. After gingerly lowering himself in his rocker, he struck a match, then cupped his gnarled hands around his pipe and lit it. He dropped the fuming match in the ashtray on the tabletop beside him. Blue-gray smoke swirled around his head as he began to rock. "Looks like a boat hit my pier," he said softly, staring down at the floor. "Probably some drunken kids from the other side of the lake. Joyriding and drinking. Hate to see what condition their *boat* is in." He took the pipe from his mouth, clamped his lips together, and shook his head. "When will they ever learn?"

Greg couldn't believe what he was hearing. Only minutes before, he had told Mr. Tucker about the attack on him and Lisa, and the subsequent damage to the pier. Apparently the old man didn't believe his story anymore than Sheriff Clifford did. Greg eyed him with contempt. *Easy. Take it easy. He's just an old man. But still, how can he sit there and tell me it was drunken kids when I just told him what happened? Who does he think he is? Old man or not, I can't just sit here and let him get away with his version of what happened out there.* Greg stood up from the sofa, grabbed a Coke. He opened it, took a swig, then leveled his eyes at the old man. "With all due respect, Mr. Tucker ... that was no damn boat!" He was trembling inside with anger. *But he would fight it, control it. Remember ... he's just an old man. Probably doesn't* mean any harm. Maybe he's senile. Maybe they *both* are. He cleared his throat, softening his tone of voice. "That was a catfish, Mr. Tucker. A *giant* catfish. A catfish so big, it destroyed your pier. So big, it ate my dog. And it probably ate your granddaughter, Rachel."

Mrs. Tucker entered the room just as Greg spoke those last words. She was carrying a large glass bowl heaping with pretzels. Apparently she was shocked by his last remark, for she gasped and dropped the bowl on the floor, shattering it. Pretzels and shards of glass scattered everywhere. At the sound of the crash, she threw her hands to her face, then froze, staring wide-eyed at the mess on the floor.

For a fleeting moment, everyone froze, the room deathly quiet.

Lisa and Jenny's entrance broke the silence.

"What happened?" Lisa asked, nonchalantly.

Even at this awkward moment, Greg couldn't help but notice how beautiful she looked in a pair of Jenny's blue jeans and white sweatshirt. He noted with interest the soft, sexy curves of her womanly figure. "It was an accident," Greg said sheepishly, averting his eyes.

"I'll get a broom and dustpan," Jenny volunteered, then disappeared into the kitchen.

Mrs. Tucker scurried to the sofa and sat down between Timmy and Tommy, her eyes brimming with tears. She sat in shocked silence, hands clapped to her flushed face. Timmy and Tommy lowered their Coke cans from their mouths and stared at her, bewildered.

"Mrs. Tuc-kor, are there any pwetzels left?" Tommy asked hopefully.

Mrs. Tucker forced a smile. "In the kitchen," she said softly, rubbing Tommy's head. "I'll get them." She started to get up.

"No, you stay put, Mrs. Tucker," Lisa said. "I'll get 'em more pretzels."

She passed Jenny on the way to the kitchen, who was carrying a broom and dustpan.

As Jenny began sweeping up the mess, Mr. Tucker jerked his pipe from his mouth, his eyebrows lowered and bristling, and pointed a bony finger at Greg.

"You mustn't talk that way about our granddaughter," he said sternly.

Greg felt guilty for having upset the kind and elderly couple. He hadn't meant to cause them any distress, and yet he had to get through to them, make them realize that something was terribly amiss on Mink Lake, and it might involve their granddaughter. He faced Mr. Tucker, took a deep breath. "I don't mean to upset you, Mr. Tucker. But you have to understand that there's a chance that Rachel may have been killed by that … that …monster."

Timmy leaned forward on the sofa, looking at Mr. Tucker. "Don't worry, it's not weally a monn-stor. It's only a giant catfish. Wight, Gweg?"

Mrs. Tucker put her arm around him and kissed the top of his head. "Shhh, Timmy," she said softly, dabbing her tears. "Drink your soda, dear."

Mr. Tucker struggled out of the rocker, clutching his pipe in a horny fist. He was glaring at Greg. "Young man, don't you dare stand there and tell us our Rachel is dead." His voice was strained and trembling, but he said it like he meant it. "Bad enough you come around here with that cock and bull story about some giant catfish. And now you want us to believe that it killed Rachel, too?" He started coughing, lowered himself back into the rocker. He cleared his throat and said, "I've heard enough of this rubbish. Rachel's not dead. She's just … missing."

"Who's Rachel?" Lisa asked, setting a plastic bowl full of pretzels on the coffee table in front of the twins. They eagerly dug in, each of them grabbing a fistful. Lisa grabbed a handful, too.

"Oh, she's our granddaughter, dear," Mrs. Tucker said with a weak smile. "She's been missing since last summer." She nodded at the tray of soft drinks on the coffee table. "Care for a soda, dear? You, too, Jenny."

"Oh, I'm sorry to hear that," Lisa said, reaching for a can of Seven-Up. "Thanks for the pop."

Having cleaned up the shattered bowl and spilled pretzels, Jenny grabbed a Coke and sat down in an upholstered chair opposite the sofa. "Thank you, Mrs. Tucker," she said quietly.

Frustrated, Greg crossed the room, stood in front of the gun cabinet, and stared at the weapons behind the glass doors. These people are driving me nuts, he thought, sipping his Coke. Talk about being in denial. Wow!

Lisa walked over to him, her can of soda in hand. He turned to face her, and she kissed him lightly on the mouth, startling him. "Thanks for saving my life tonight."

"You're welcome."

"I owe you an apology, Greg."

"What for?"

"For not believing you about the giant catfish. I thought the whole thing was just a big joke, or a big mistake. I figured you probably saw a large fish in the water and then—out of fear or panic—you just kind of exaggerated the whole story."

He grabbed her arm and pulled her into the hallway, out of earshot from the others. "Now you sound like Mr. Tucker," he said softly. "I didn't exaggerate *anything.*"

"Well, not on purpose for heaven's sake. But sometimes people do stretch the truth a little when they're scared and under a lot of stress, you know. Anyway, I know *now* you weren't exaggerating at all. And I'm sorry I didn't believe you in the first place." Slowly, suggestively, she traced her index finger around the rim of the Seven-Up can, eyeing him slyly. "Are we still friends?" she asked fawningly. A mischievous smile rippled across her lips, her eyes flashing.

That was too much for Greg. How could he possibly resist her? The answer was simple—he couldn't! He pulled her close and kissed her with burning desire.

When the kiss ended, they stared lovingly into each other's eyes. "Yeah ... I guess we're still friends," Lisa said jokingly.

Greg smiled briefly, then frowned, his face suddenly serious. "I just don't understand why the Tuckers refuse to believe us. They can't possibly believe that you and Jenny and the twins and I are all lying about that ... that *thing* out there, can they?"

"Well, they *are* old," she whispered.

Ignoring that excuse, Greg lowered his voice and said, "And look at the way he snapped at me when I mentioned Rachel's name. It's like he completely refuses to believe that there's even the slightest chance that she may be dead."

"Wouldn't you?" she asked matter-of-factly. "If you were an old, frail man, and your granddaughter was missing for a year—a granddaughter whom he obviously loved very much—would you want to accept the fact that she may be dead after all this time of hoping and praying for her safe return? Think about it. Would you be able to accept the possibility that she had been devoured by a giant catfish? That you would never see her again—dead or alive? That you wouldn't even be able to bury her corpse, lay her to rest? Think about it."

"Okay, okay. I get your point." He leveled his eyes at her, his face grave. "I'm gonna have to kill it—before it kills one of us."

Lisa was taken aback, her eyes wide with alarm. "You? *You* can't kill it."

"The heck I can't."

"How?"

He stepped in front of the gun cabinet and pointed to the AK-47. "With this."

She stared at him incredulously. Keeping her voice low, she said, "I don't think Mr. Tucker is going to give you his permission to use that thing."

Greg glanced over at the old man, who was sitting in his rocking chair, puffing on his pipe. He was chatting and chuckling with the twins, who were sitting cross-legged on the floor at his feet. Apparently he was telling them a story as they stared up at him in wonder, resting their elbows on their knees and supporting their chins on little fists. "Then I'll take it without his permission," he whispered. "First thing tomorrow morning, I'll sneak out of here with the rifle. Then I'm gonna hunt that thing down, and I'm gonna kill it once and for all."

"And just how do you think Sheriff Clifford will react to *that?* You out on the lake with an AK-47! Come on, Greg—think!"

"To hell with him! He had his chance to help me, but he wasn't the least bit interested. So now it's up to *me* to do his job."

"I'm going with you."

"Oh, no you're not!" he said firmly, raising his voice slightly. "You were almost killed tonight. Isn't once enough? Next time you may not be so lucky."

"Okay, wait. I don't think you quite understand. I didn't *ask* if I could go with you. I *said* I'm going with you."

He started to object, but she quickly cut him off.

"Now you know you can't drive a boat and"—she nodded

at the deadly-looking rifle behind the glass—"shoot that thing at the same time. I'm going with and that's all there is to it." She turned and started to walk away, then went back over to him and kissed him on the cheek. "See you in the morning, beautiful." To the others she said, "Goodnight, everybody."

They all smiled, wished her good night, and Mr. Tucker said, "Thank you for fixing my truck, young lady. Mrs. Tucker will write you a check for the parts, plus a little something extra for your trouble."

"You're quite welcome, Mr. Tucker," she said, heading toward the stairs. "But please pay me for the parts only. I don't want anything for my labor—it was my pleasure," she said coyly. She glanced at Greg and smiled radiantly. "It really was." She turned and went upstairs.

Later that night, after everyone had gone to bed, Greg tossed and turned on the sofa. Terrifying visions of the giant catfish attacking him and Lisa kept filling his head. Finally, he fell asleep and dreamed only of Lisa—beautiful, spunky Lisa.

The next morning, Greg woke up at five o'clock with the sun streaming in his face. Instantly he was out of bed, scrambling for his clothes. Today was the day. Today he would kill the monster catfish, once and for all. Then he would tow its giant carcass to shore for everyone to see, including Sheriff Clifford. Can't wait to see the look on that idiot sheriff's face then, he thought, gloating.

He forced himself to tiptoe quietly up the stairs. He stole into Jenny's room, who was sharing her bed with Lisa. He gingerly kissed Lisa on the lips, waking her. Then, while she got dressed, he crept downstairs to the living room and carefully removed the AK-47 from the gun cabinet.

The weapon was heavy and awkward, like no other gun

he had ever handled before. The very design and feel of it spelled death and destruction. He recalled Mr. Tucker's words regarding the rifle: "She can shoot holes right through steel piping, concrete blocks, wooden posts ... you name it!" Holding the deadly weapon in his hands, caressing the cold steel barrel and the thick wooden stock, Greg didn't doubt its potential power.

Gently, delicately, as if it were a bomb about to explode, he laid the gun on the sofa, then returned to the gun cabinet for the ammo clip and bullets. His heart sank when he discovered the bottom compartment was locked. Of course, you idiot! Don't you remember? Mr. Tucker had said that he always kept the ammunition locked up. He had forgotten all about it. Worse still, he didn't know where the key was kept. Nice going, stupid. Now what are you going to do? Wake up the old man and ask him for the key? Jesus! Kneeling on the floor, he was stooped over, fidgeting with the lock. A light sweat coated his forehead. He tugged on the small doors, but the lock held fast. "Darn!" he muttered, wiping a hand across his brow.

Suddenly, out of nowhere, Lisa whispered behind. "Ready?"

It scared the hell out of him, and he jumped, bumping his head against the oak cabinet. "Ow!"

"Shhh! You'll wake the others," she whispered. She knelt beside him, dressed in Jenny's jeans and sweatshirt. "What's wrong?"

"It's locked—what do you *think* is wrong?" he snapped, but managed to keep his voice low.

She jerked her head back, frowning at him. "Jeez ...aren't we crabby this morning?"

"Sorry," he whispered. "But I don't have a *darn* key, and the *darn* bullets are locked inside the *darn* cabinet!"

She glanced at the brass lock, fingered it, then leaned over and whispered in his ear. "Guess what? You don't need a *darn* key to open the *darn* cabinet to get the *darn* bullets." She kissed his ear lightly, then stood up. "Be right back."

He watched her scurry out of the room, feeling stupid and dumbfounded. Now what's she up to?

Moments later, she returned with a nail file. "I borrowed this from Jenny. It was lying on top of her dresser." She knelt beside him and inserted the file into the lock.

"You're dumber than I am," he said incredulously. "You can't open a lock with that flimsy—"

CLICK!

The small wooded door popped open, revealing boxes of ammunition and an assortment of ammo clips.

"You were saying?" she said smugly, a smile tugging at the corners of her mouth. "Don't be so surprised. I told you I was mechanical."

* * *

Later, cruising the lake inside Mr. Tucker's speedboat, Greg cradled the loaded AK-47 in his arms, his eyes glued to the rippled water, waiting, watching, every muscle in his body tense with anticipation.

As per Greg's instructions, Lisa steered the boat in shallow water along the shoreline, keeping it at a crawl. "Why begin our search in the shallows?" she asked. "Wouldn't you have a better chance of finding a giant catfish in *deep* water?"

"So far all of the attacks have occurred in shallow water," he answered, his eyes scanning the surface on all sides of the boat. "My guess is that it feeds in the shallows at night and early morning. During the day it probably moves into deeper water. So just keep it moving nice and slow. I'm gonna nail that thing as soon as it pops its ugly head up."

"What if it doesn't show up?"

"It'll show." He checked the rifle's safety button. The safety was on.

"How can you be sure?"

"Because I've been here only two days, and already the thing has attacked me twice. Don't worry ... it'll show." He checked the ammo clip. It was full.

"Well, I don't know. It's a pretty big lake. We may be out here for hours and never *see* the thing. Maybe it's done feeding for the morning. And maybe it's already moved into deeper water. Maybe we should—"

"Look," he interrupted, "unless you have a better plan, will you please just drive the boat and be quiet?"

"My ...we *are* crabby this morning—aren't we?"

He sighed, taking his eyes off the water just long enough to roll them.

"It just so happens, Sherlock, I *DO* have a better plan. We should be dragging some bait behind the boat like they did in that movie *Jaws*. We have to make that thing come to us, lure it, entice it with some kind of bait.

Preferably *stinky* bait. Any kind of dead fish would probably do the trick."

He was stunned. She's right, you know. She's *always* right. He pressed his lips tightly together, trying to keep from grinning.

"Well?" she asked, waiting for his response.

His face burst into a huge smile. "Why didn't *I* think of that?"

"Hey! That's what I'm here for. You just do the shooting, and I'll take care of everything else!"

He chuckled, shook his head, never taking his eyes off the water. "I apologize for being crabby. Guess I'm a little stressed."

"Yeah, well ... just be glad you're not a girl."

They both laughed.

"So where do we get the bait?" she asked, steering their boat as it chugged past a weed-choked bay.

Greg noticed a lone fisherman sitting in a twelve-foot, aluminum rowboat. "Let's talk to that guy. See if he's caught any fish yet. Maybe he'll give us one to use for bait."

The man's boat was anchored in the small pocket of water amidst a carpet of lily pads. He was sitting with his back to Lisa and Greg, casting a surface plug toward the shoreline. There were no cabins on this part of the lake. The shoreline was overgrown with jack pine, scrub oak, and a tangled mass of underbrush.

The man turned and looked at them, grinning. He was fifty-ish, wearing a tan cap and matching tan vest. A small assortment of colorful lures hung from his vest pockets, the silvery hooks glittering in the early-morning sun.

"Mornin'," he said. A cigarette dangling from his mouth wobbled when he spoke.

"Good morning," Lisa replied, smiling. She stopped their boat's engine.

Greg was lowering the weapon out of sight just as the man had turned to face them. Hope he didn't see it, Greg thought, forcing a smile. Don't want to scare the daylights out of him. Probably think I was some kind of psychopath or something. Who wouldn't? Not a whole lot of people out here patrolling the lake with an AK-47.

He shaded his brow with his hand, squinting against the sun's glare. "Any luck?" he asked cordially.

"Yeah! You bet!" the man blurted, laying his pole across his lap, the line going limp. He reached over the side of the boat with both hands and hefted a stringer of fish from the water. "Caught these beauties in half an hour," he said, beaming. "One right after the other. Ain't never seen nothin' like it!"

Greg's eyes popped from his head, his mouth hanging to his knees. "Holy cow!" Thrashing on the end of the stringer were three of the largest northern pike he had ever seen. These were not the usual one-pound "snakes" that everyone frequently caught. These pike were enormous, long and heavy-bodied, each one weighing perhaps twelve to fifteen pounds. Their slick, white bellies glistened in the sunlight. Greg gaped in disbelief, his mind struggling to comprehend what he was seeing. He was seeing the unbelievable.

The man was obviously elated. "I've been fishing this lake for twenty-seven years, and I ain't never seen nothin' like *this* before." He dropped the fish back into the water with a loud splash. The other end of the stringer was fastened to an oarlock. The metal chain strained and scraped against the boat with a sharp metallic sound, as the trophy fish churned and thrashed below. "Must be the oxygen in the water," he said, picking up his pole. He reeled in some slack line. "Makes 'em grow like hell."

"Holy cow!" Greg cried again, his mind still numb, and the man chuckled. Suddenly Greg yearned for his own fishing pole. The heck with this stupid search, he thought. Probably just a waste of time anyway. After all, I *am* on vacation. He recalled with empathy the bumper sticker he had seen several times back home while stuck in traffic: I'D RATHER BE FISHING! "What kind of lure did you u—"

A small eruption in the lily pads made Greg jerk his head up, just in time to see yet another enormous pike inhale the man's surface plug.

"Oooo-wee!" the man shouted, jumping to his feet. He leaned back hard against the line, setting the hook. The pike exploded through the pads, its flaming red gills flared, shaking its head violently in an effort to throw the hook. But its ferocious outburst did nothing more than fling flecks of water and lily pads from its mouth. The hook held fast, enabling the man to coax the pike back to the boat.

"Jeez!" Greg cried. To Lisa he said, "Did you see that? Unbelievable!"

"What is it?" she cried, excited. "What did he catch?"

"It's a pike!" Greg said, his heart thudding with excitement. "Looks like another whopper!" He watched the man grab a net with one hand and lean over, his back to them, trying to net the big fish. After a lot of splashing and what seemed to be an eternity, the man scooped the fish and hoisted it up out of the water with one hand, clutching his pole with the other.

"Another big one!" the man called over his shoulder. "Must be at least fifteen p—"

An explosion ripped through the water beneath the dangling pike. It was the giant catfish, blasting skyward, its gaping maw engulfing the pike, the net, and the man's hand before sliding back beneath the green canopy of lily pads.

The man shrieked, clutching what was left of his arm. He stumbled backwards, horrified at the bloody stump, and fell overboard. The creature was on him in a second, swallowing his legs first, then biting him in half at the waist. Blood spewed from his shredded waist, coloring the water around him dark red.

"Holy—!" Greg screamed, jerking the rifle to his shoulder. He flicked the safety off, then squeezed the trigger without aiming. POP! POP! POP! All three shots were high, missing the monster completely, piercing the man's boat, instead, in the bow, high above the water line. The recoil was tremendous. Despite Mr. Tucker's previous warning (" ...hold on to your hat, 'cause she kicks like a son-of-a-gun!"), Greg hadn't expected such a violent kick. His shoulder throbbed with pain. Ignoring Lisa's screams, his heart hammering, he forced himself to take careful aim. This time he was able to line his sights up on the patch of water next to the man, waiting for the creature's head to appear.

The man blinked his eyes and worked his mouth as if gasping for air. But no sound escaped his lips. The last thing Greg saw before the monster exploded through the surface and swallowed the upper torso bobbing in the bloody water was cold, stark terror on the man's face.

POP! POP! POP! POP! POP! POP! POP! POP! POP! POP!

All ten shots ripped into the creature's flesh before it slid beneath the surface.

"I got it!" Greg yelled, his eyes wild. He shot a glance at Lisa. "Did you see it?" he squealed, his voice charged with emotion. "I got him! I got him!"

Lisa was drained, her face a ghastly white. "Did you kill it?" she asked, her voice quivering. Her eyes were shimmering with tears. "Is it dead?"

"It has to be! I shot him ten times! Ten times, Lisa! I got that sucker ten times! With this!" He thrust the AK-47 above his head, clutching it in both hands, shaking it victoriously. "Whoo-weee! I told you I—"

CRASH!

The giant catfish slammed into the side of their boat, knocking the rifle out of Greg's hands. Greg heard the AK-47 splash into the lake as his knees buckled under him from the shattering blow. He crumpled to the floor of the boat, stunned. Lisa's screams brought him quickly to his feet. She was still seated behind the driver's seat, her face etched in sheer panic. She was screaming and pointing at the water.

Greg snapped his head in the direction of her point and was horror-struck when he saw the creature buzzing through the water, its long, ugly whiskers pressed flat against its flanks, heading straight for their boat. Greg just had time to brace himself before the creature rammed them. The jarring blow rattled his teeth, and he heard the sickening sound of wood splintering. "Oh, no!" He watched in horror as the monster resurfaced several yards away, then began another attack. "Lisa, start the boat! Start it now!"

CRASH!

His heart racing wildly, thudding in his chest, he saw Lisa pounce on the control panel and wrench the ignition key. The motor coughed and sputtered, but it wouldn't start. The strong odor of gasoline wafted in the air.

"What's wrong?" he shouted, scrambling to the driver's seat. He stood behind her, leaning over her, his hands clenched.

"I DON'T KNOW!" she screamed, tears running down her cheeks. She gritted her teeth, squeezing the key between her thumb and index finger. She twisted the key to the right until her knuckles turned white. Again the motor coughed and sputtered. But it wouldn't start. "COME ON!" she screamed. "COME ON!"

And then Greg saw it—the red needle inside the glass dome on the gas gage was pointing to "EMPTY." "We're out of gas!" he cried, his heart sinking.

"But how? We had plenty when we started," Lisa wailed.

The smell of gasoline was overwhelming.

"Look!" Greg cried, pointing to a slick of rainbow colors floating on the surface behind their boat. "The gas is leaking! It must've cut the fuel line when it rammed us!"

CRASH!

The boat shuddered, and the sharp crack of wood splintering filled Greg's ears. A moment later, he felt something cold and wet at his feet. A sickening wave of dread washed over him when he looked down and saw water leaking into the boat, swirling over his shoes, soaking the bottom of his jeans.

Lisa gasped and clapped her hands to her face, her eyes wild with alarm. "Dear God, help us!" she squeaked.

CHAPTER 6

The boat listed precariously as water gushed through a splintered gash on the port side.

Greg saw the monster slip beneath the surface after the last attack, then resurface on the port side again, about 100 yards from the boat. "Lisa, get up on the bow!" he shouted, resisting the ever-increasing urge to panic, to scream for help. But he knew that to panic now would only seal their doom. He must keep his wits about him if they were to survive. Besides, there was no one in sight, no one who could possibly help them. He and Lisa were home all alone with death banging on their door.

The chilly lake water surged around Greg's knees, and he realized there could be no more than a minute left before the boat sank completely. As he climbed up on the bow next to Lisa, he was surprised to see that she was panic-stricken. Up until now, she had been a rock, a model of cold, rugged confidence. He recalled how only yesterday she had told off Sheriff Clifford in his office. That took a lot of guts, and he admired her for it.

But now as Greg huddled next to her, watching her tremble and cling to the bow's railing, her eyes wild with terror, her face drained of all color, he realized she was probably every bit as fragile and vulnerable as any other human being. He felt sick inside, his heart aching for her. He shouldn't have allowed her to come out here in the first place. What was he thinking? He'd give anything to whisk her away from the deadly danger they now faced. Please, God, he thought, wrapping a protective arm around her, don't let anything happen to her. Please.

"What are we going to do, Greg?" she asked, her voice quivering.

He saw the monster approaching fast on the port side, streaking beneath the surface like a deadly torpedo. He saw, too, that the bow of the boat was only a foot out of the water now, and sinking fast.

Eyeing the dead fisherman's aluminum boat anchored fifty feet off their starboard side, Greg said, "There's only one thing we *can* do—swim to the other boat."

Lisa jerked her head around, staring at him in disbelief. "You're insane!" she yelled, wide-eyed, gripping the railing with both hands. Apparently she had no intention of ever letting go.

"Trust me," he said, prying her hands loose. Then, holding her hand, he stood up and shouted, "NOW!" He felt the bow slip beneath the surface just as they dove into the water.

When they hit the water, Greg let go of her hand so she could swim. Lisa thrust her head out of the water and screamed. "Swim, Lisa," he called over his shoulder, slicing through the water toward the other boat, not daring to look back. "Swim as fast as you can." He reached the boat within seconds, then scrambled up the side and let himself drop to the floor, rolling in a pool of the dead fisherman's blood—a result of the fisherman's hand having been bitten off.

Lisa was right behind Greg, clinging to the side of the boat, panting wildly.

Greg pulled her up just as the monster glided directly beneath the boat.

"Sit on the floor!" he yelled, scrambling toward the rear of the boat. He pulled up the anchor, then started the outboard motor with one pull of the cord. He shoved the gear into forward, then cranked the throttle open.

The boat lurched forward and roared away, leaving the grisly scene behind.

Greg steered the boat toward Lisa's cabin where they could use either her phone, car, or speedboat to get help. After the fiasco with the AK-47, he realized more than ever he would need *professional* help to get the monster. His first plan of action would be to call Sheriff Clifford and convince him to get his butt out here on the double! *This* time, Greg would not take no for an answer! If he had to, he would drive to town and bring the sheriff back.

But when they reached Lisa's dock, Greg was surprised when he saw a patrol car in Lisa's driveway behind her Mustang. "Look," he said to Lisa, pointing past the pier and up the hill at the squad car.

"That's Sheriff Clifford's car," she said. "What's *he* doing here?"

"I don't know," Greg said, watching the sheriff climb out of the patrol car and start down the hill. "But his timing is perfect!" Greg eased the boat alongside the pier, cut the motor, then tied the bow to the pier. He helped Lisa out of the boat, then held her hands in his. "You okay?" he asked, brushing wet hair from her eyes.

"I'll be all right," she said, her voice still shaky. Even in soaking wet clothes, her figure was shapely and attractive.

Sheriff Clifford stood on the end of the pier behind them, his hands on his hips, a cigar jutting from his mouth, staring at the two of them.

"Boy, are we glad to see you!" Greg said, approaching the big lawman. But no sooner did those words leave his lips than a sense of foreboding swept over him. He didn't know why, didn't know what it was that brought on this sense of dread. He studied Sheriff Clifford carefully. Maybe it was the way the sheriff was staring at Lisa in her wet, clinging clothes.

The sheriff's eyes met Greg's, and he just stood there, staring for a beat. Finally he snatched the cigar from his mouth and held it between two thick fingers. "Someone called in that they heard shots fired and some screaming on the lake. Said it was a couple of kids—a young man and woman—doing all the shooting." He jabbed the cigar between his lips and squinted. "I figured it was you two. Wanna tell me about it?"

While Greg excitedly explained to the sheriff the terror that had just unfolded on Mink Lake, Sheriff Clifford glanced at Greg's bloodstained clothes, then kept his eyes glued on Lisa.

His staring must've made Lisa feel very uncomfortable, for she abruptly interrupted Greg's story to excuse herself and change her clothes.

Greg became annoyed when he saw that the sheriff's eyes were following Lisa all the way up the hill to her cabin. What a jerk, he thought. He's not listening to a word I'm saying. When Greg finished his story, Lisa joined them on the pier again, wearing a red sweatshirt, jeans, and a pair of sneakers. Her hair was pulled back into a fresh ponytail, and Greg noticed the mascara that had streaked earlier down her face had been wiped clean. In a matter of only a few minutes, Lisa was beautiful again. Greg smiled and held her hand.

Sheriff Clifford stepped inside the fisherman's boat and examined the blood-splattered interior, his brow lowered, his face stern. Puffs of gray, acrid smoke bellowed from his lips, his cigar lolling from one corner of his mouth to the other. He examined the bullet holes in the bow. Then, kneeling on one of the aluminum boat seats, he stooped over and dabbed at the pooled blood on the floor with a finger. He stared at it in silence for a few moments.

"That blood is from the guy's hand being bitten off," Greg offered.

"We tried to tell you yesterday about that giant catfish," Lisa scolded the sheriff. "But you wouldn't listen to us. Now there's a dead man out there."

Sheriff Clifford wiped his finger on his trousers, then stepped from the boat up onto the dock. "Catfish, huh? If that was a catfish, I'll eat my badge," he sneered, flicking cigar ashes into the lake. "More than likely this blood is from gunshot wounds." He shoved the cigar between his teeth and planted himself firmly in front of Greg, towering over him. "More than likely, you shot a poor, defenseless fisherman. "Then you went and dumped his body in the lake."

Greg's mouth fell to his knees, speechless. He couldn't believe his ears. Surely the sheriff wasn't serious. He must be kidding him, teasing him. He's just trying to give me a hard time, Greg thought. He can't really believe I shot and killed that guy. Greg waited for the sheriff to smile, to offer some clue that he was only kidding.

Sheriff Clifford did *not* smile. "Where's the weapon?" he asked, dead serious.

"I-I-I told you," Greg stammered. "It fell in the lake when that monster rammed our boat." His sense of dread told him that things were not going well. A knot formed in his stomach, twisting, churning. His heart thumped in his chest, and his mouth was dry as cotton.

"Yeah, sure, kid" the sheriff scoffed. "And I'm the tooth fairy." He blew a puff of smoke from his mouth, eyes squinted, hands on hips.

"YOU KNOW DARN WELL WE DIDN'T SHOOT ANYBODY!" Lisa shrieked, her face growing red with rage.

"Why in the world would we do that?" Greg asked, trying to control his own temper. He sensed that he and Lisa were in big trouble, even though they had done nothing wrong. He had had just about enough of this buffoon with a badge.

"Robbery," the sheriff answered simply.

"WHAT ARE YOU TALKING ABOUT!" Lisa shrieked again, veins popping in her temples.

"Why in the world would we rob anybody?" Greg asked, helplessly. He could feel the situation growing more and more hopeless, his anger giving way to fear. In the back of his mind, he wondered where he and Lisa could go for help— *real* help. It was becoming more and more apparent that Sheriff Clifford would be of no help to them at all.

"Drug money," Sheriff Clifford replied. "You needed money for drugs, so you shot and killed that fisherman, took his money, and dumped his body in the lake. Seems pretty cut and dried to me."

Lisa thrust herself past Greg, almost lunging at the sheriff, glaring at him, her chin jutting up at him defiantly. "You know darn well I don't do drugs!" she hissed, her face wild. "And neither does Greg! And besides, whoever heard of robbing a fisherman? What would be the point? A fisherman doesn't carry a lot of money. How much money do *you* take when you go fishing, Sheriff?"

"Tell it to the judge," Sheriff Clifford said arrogantly. He removed a pair of handcuffs from his belt, then looked menacingly at Greg. "Turn around and put you hands behind your back, son. You're under arrest for first degree murder."

"Murder!" Greg cried. "You can't arrest me—you don't even have a body!"

Sheriff Clifford sighed deeply then said, "Son ... I told you to turn around."

Shocked, speechless, Greg obeyed.

"You're insane!" Lisa cried. "I'm calling the state police!" She turned and started marching toward her cabin, but the sheriff grabbed her arm and yanked her back. "It don't work that way, sweetheart," he said, snapping a pair of cuffs around her wrists before she could resist him. Then he spun her around, leering at her. "You're under arrest, too. Accessory to murder."

* * *

Hours later, at the jail, each of them locked inside their own cells, Greg tried to comfort Lisa, talking soothingly to her through the thick iron bars that separated them. "Come on, Lisa ... don't cry. We'll get out of this mess ... somehow."

She was sitting on the edge of a thin, lumpy cot tucked in a corner of her cell. Greg noticed the cot was exactly like the one in his cell: old and filthy, stained with God only knew what. And it reeked, too—smelling of sweat and urine.

She sobbed softly, her face buried in her hands. "How are we ever going to get out of this?" she cried. She raised her head, her eyes red and shimmering with tears. "The sheriff is nuts, and we're trapped here. Nobody even knows we're here—except for him. I'm scared, Greg. I don't trust him."

It broke Greg's heart to see her crying, hurting. She looked so helpless crouching in the corner, a prisoner inside Sheriff Clifford's creepy jail, and he was dreadfully afraid for her. She was right, of course. No one knew they were here except that slob of a sheriff. He pressed his face against the bars, watching her with tender eyes. "Come here," he said softly.

She rose and went to him, wiping tears away with her fingertips. "What?" she asked in a squeaky voice.

He grabbed her hands through the bars and held them, while gazing deeply into her eyes. "We *will* get out of this," he said confidently. "I promise." Though he didn't have a clue as to *how* they would get out of it, he was fiercely determined, nevertheless.

She sighed deeply, forced a trace smile. "I just wish we had never gotten into this mess in the first place. I wish—"

"You wish you had never met me," Greg interrupted, feeling responsible for their predicament.

Her gaze dropped to the floor. "I didn't say that."

"You didn't have to," he replied sheepishly. "I guess I really screwed things up for you. I'm sorry I got you mixed up in all this. If you had never met me, you wouldn't be here right now." He let his forehead rest against the steel bar, thinking. "I should've just gone to the sheriff by myself with this giant catfish story. You didn't have to be involved at all."

"But I *am* involved …in more ways than one," she said, gaining her composure. "I love you, Greg Nelson."

Her words melted him, moving him deeply. He swallowed hard, trying to suppress the growing lump in his throat. "I-I love you, too," he said, his eyes misting. "Too bad we couldn't have met under different circumstances. Believe me …if I could do it over, I would, and I'd leave you out of it."

"That isn't important, Greg." She took a deep breath, lifted her chin. "I'm all right. Really. And I'm *very* glad I met you. None of this is your fault. You're the victim in this mess, not the villain."

Her words soothed him, and he suddenly realized *she* was comforting *him*. "Thanks. But just the same, I'm sorry I got you mixed up in all this." He felt powerless, frustrated. There was nothing to say to her to erase his guilt.

"What about this giant catfish business?" Lisa asked. "I mean, what in the world is going on here? Where'd it come from? How'd it get so big in the first place. Mink Lake has been here for thousands of years, and there's never been a giant catfish before."

Greg chewed his lip for a moment, pondering. "I don't know," he said, stroking his chin. "But I noticed *all* the fish in this lake are bigger than usual this year. Much bigger."

"Yeah, but what's causing it?"

"I don't know," he answered. "But I'll tell you one thing— I bet the Tuckers' granddaughter, Rachel, became prey for that monster out there, and that's why she disappeared last year." His face suddenly puckered. "Except *that* doesn't explain what happened to her car."

"Yeah," Lisa agreed, "there's no way that catfish could've eaten her car. That monster isn't *that* big."

"Maybe someone stole her car after she had been killed by the catfish."

"That's possible." She shuddered. "The whole thing gives me the creeps. It's just horrible."

"Yeah, and the worst part is, there's no way to prove any of it ever happened because there'd be nothing left of her. No body. No bones. Nothing." He stared at her hard, his face pinched. "Is there anything different about the lake this year? Anything new around the lake?"

"What do you mean?" she asked, puzzled.

He thought about Dad's pesticides and all those hundreds of exterminators at the pest control convention that Dad and Mom were attending. "You know—like a factory or something? Something that may be dumping chemicals into the lake?"

Lisa's eyes lit up instantly. "Wait a minute!" she cried, squeezing his hands. "I remember reading a while back about that nuclear power plant up near Pine Acres that had to be shut down. Something about radiation leaking into the Wolverine River."

"What! My dad said he heard they shut it down because it was cheaper to burn coal."

Lisa shrugged. "Maybe it's some kind of government cover-up or something—like they do with UFO's."

"Doesn't the Wolverine River flow through Mink Lake?" Greg asked, his mind beginning to churn.

"Yes it does," Lisa replied. "Do you think the radiation could still be leaking into Mink Lake, and it's causing everything to grow so big?"

"Holy cow!" Greg cried. "It could be. For science class last year, I had to do a report on the Chernobyl disaster of 1986. I came across an article in *Time* magazine about the aftereffects of the radiation. They had photos of farm animals that were deformed because of the radiation: pigs with no eyes, colts with eight legs, and calves with no mouths."

"Gross!" Lisa said, wriggling her nose.

"Yeah," Greg agreed. "And get this—the article had pictures of some kind of fish that live in the cooling reservoir of the Chernobyl plant. It said that those fish were growing much larger than normal since the meltdown."

"Oh, my god, Greg!" she cried. "That means there's documented proof that radiation can cause fish to grow bigger than normal."

"*Much* bigger," he added.

"Then we have to tell the sheriff!" she blurted, bouncing with renewed enthusiasm. "If we can get him to listen to our story, then maybe he'll finally do something about it. We can't just sit here like this. There's a monster out there and it's killing innocent people!"

"There may be more than one," Greg reminded her. "There

could be a whole school of giant catfish swimming around out there—although it's not likely because nobody has reported seeing even one of them that we know of."

"How do we know that somebody else hasn't already complained to Sheriff Clifford about seeing a giant catfish, and he just chose to ignore it—just like he's doing with us?"

The thick wooden door that separated the sheriff's office from the jail section in the rear of the building screeched open. Sheriff Clifford staggered through the doorway, holding an empty liquor bottle by its neck.

"Speak of the devil," Greg said in a low voice.

The sheriff lumbered over to Lisa's cell and stopped outside the iron bar door. He removed a set of keys from his waistband and fumbled with them in the door's lock. A moment later, the tumbler clicked open, and the sheriff stepped inside Lisa's cell. He reached behind him with his free hand and pulled the cell door closed. The heavy steel door clanged shut. The sheriff stood silently, swaying from side to side, staring at Lisa.

Greg immediately noticed an evil gleam in the sheriff's eye, and cold panic exploded in his gut. He clung tighter to Lisa's hands. "When do we get to see the judge?" he asked, his voice dry and trembling. He was trying to get Sheriff Clifford's mind off of Lisa. And at the same time, he didn't want to show any fear. Something in his gut told him that Sheriff Clifford was the kind of man who preyed on fearful people.

Sheriff Clifford grinned, revealing yellow and broken teeth. He took a swig from the empty bottle, realized it was empty, then whipped it to the floor. The bottle smashed on the rough concrete, spraying shards of glass across the floor.

Lisa jumped and spun around, facing the sheriff, her hands clenched into small fists.

Greg felt his heart leap into his throat, his pulse running wild.

Sheriff Clifford lumbered over to the small cot in the corner, towered over it. He looked at it, then set his eyes on Lisa. "I *am* the judge," he said, his speech slightly slurred. "Judge, jury, and executioner." His eyes still clung to Lisa. "And anything else you want me to be. Hey, heh, heh."

Greg saw that the drunken hulk was drooling now. Got to do something, he thought with increasing dread.

Apparently Lisa had sensed something dreadful was unfolding, too, for she quickly tried to steer the sheriff's thoughts off of her and unto the giant catfish. "Listen, Sheriff. We figured out what's causing the fish to grow so big in Mink Lake. We know where that giant catfish came fro"—

Sheriff Clifford swaggered over to Lisa, his shoes squeaking beneath his tremendous weight. He loomed over her, panting, his bloodshot eyes gleaming.

Standing only a couple of feet away, separated by the iron bars, Greg could smell the stench of stale alcohol fuming from the sheriff's mouth and flared nostrils.

"Stay away from me," Lisa ordered, backing into the bars.

Suddenly the sheriff lunged at her, grabbing her wrists, pulling her away from the cell wall and away from Greg.

Lisa cried out in alarm. "Don't touch me!" she screamed, struggling to get away.

Sheriff Clifford squealed with delight, as he continued pulling her. "LET HER GO!" Greg shouted through clenched teeth. "WHAT'S WRONG WITH YOU! LET HER GO!"

The sheriff giggled with excitement, spittle drooling down his chin.

Unable to wrestle free from his iron grip, Lisa sank her teeth into the sheriff's hand, causing him to release her instantly. With her hands now free, she buried her fingertips into his eyes and raked downward, screaming at him like a woman gone mad. She darted back to Greg, who was fiercely clutching the bars that separated them, shouting at the top of his lungs.

Ignoring Greg, Sheriff Clifford glared at Lisa. "You'll pay for that!" Then he lunged at her again, but this time she was able to duck in time, just missing his big hands.

The sheriff spun around to face her again, turning his back on Greg.

Apparently the sheriff's threat triggered in Lisa a primal instinct of survival, for she now fought with a new savagery. She leaped at the sheriff, trying to gouge his eyes again. But this time, he caught both her wrists in his massive hands. With lightning speed, she kicked her knee upward, ramming it hard into the sheriff's groin.

Sheriff Clifford cried out in pain and stumbled back against the bars, almost smashing his back into Greg's face.

Greg instinctively slipped his arm around the bull neck and squeezed it as hard as he could. He gouged his bony forearm deep into the sheriff's throat, choking him, smashing his huge head against the hard steel.

But the maniacal sheriff struggled with crazed intensity, smacking his saucer-sized hands against the bars, trying to reach behind and above his head, his thick fingers only inches from Greg's face. The more Sheriff Clifford struggled, the more Greg could feel his grip weaken.

Greg's mind reeled with terror. What if he let go? The sheriff would be in a frenzy, bent on harming Lisa. I can't let go, he thought. No matter what. Gotta hold on. Hold on.

Gasping, the sheriff jerked and twisted with amazing strength. In his frantic struggling, the butt of his revolver clanked against the steel bars.

With his free hand, Greg reached through the bars and

grabbed the gun, drawing it out of its holster, only to have it knocked from his hand when the sheriff tried to take it from him. The .357 magnum revolver clattered on the floor at the sheriff's feet.

Greg tried to scoop the gun into his cell, using his foot. But the sheriff was quicker, and he kicked the gun further inside Lisa's cell, out of Greg's reach.

Lisa pounced on the gun, then snatched it up, ducking away from the sheriff's flailing hands. Standing up, she cocked the gun and pointed it at Sheriff Clifford. "Give me the keys," she hissed. "Or so help me—I'll blow your ugly head off!"

Greg knew from the tone of her voice that she meant it.

Apparently the sheriff knew it, too, for he quickly dug the keys from his waistband and tossed them to her.

Picking up the keys, she went to the door, tried several keys until the right one finally unlocked the door, then stepped outside the cell and slammed the door shut behind her.

Seeing that she was safe, Greg released his hold on Sheriff Clifford, then stepped away from the bars.

Sheriff Clifford clutched his throat, coughing and gagging. His face was a shocking red, his eyes wild. "I'll get you for this!" he hissed, glaring at Greg. Then he glared at Lisa, who was unlocking Greg's cell. "I'll get you, too, sweetheart."

"Don't count on it," Greg said, feeling a bit cocky now that the sheriff was safely locked up. "We're going to the state police. I'm sure they'll be very interested to know what kind of sheriff you are."

"And I'm sure they'll want to know about that giant catfish, too," Lisa added.

At that the sheriff leaped against the bars with renewed savagery, arms flailing, fists slicing the air, his face contorted with uncontrollable rage. "I'LL KILL YOU!" he screamed. "I'LL KILL YOU BOTH!"

The verbal assault unnerved Greg. He was so shocked, so shaken by the savage outburst, he felt like vomiting. Every nerve in his body surged with adrenaline. He had never seen such violence, such insanity from another human being before. But then, Sheriff Clifford was obviously not just another human being. What kind of sheriff attacks his prisoners and makes threats against their lives? Suddenly he realized he was dealing with *two* monsters—one with whiskers and one with a badge. "Let's get out of here," he said, taking Lisa's hand. "This guy is psycho."

CHAPTER 7

Using the phone in the sheriff's office, Greg called the state police headquarters in Madison. The dispatcher switched him to an Inspector Gramms of the homicide department. It hadn't even occurred to Greg that the death of the fisherman was exactly that—a homicide. He was surprised and relieved to find Inspector Gramms was an easy man to talk to. Inspector Gramms was soft-spoken and mild-mannered, yet he had a distinct air of authority about him. Greg pictured him as being small in stature, but big in principles. Greg liked him, respected him right from the start. While Greg related his story to Inspector Gramms, Greg could hear Sheriff Clifford in back still screaming and cussing.

Apparently Inspector Gramms could hear the commotion, too, over the phone. "Who's that?" he asked Greg.

"That's Sheriff Clifford," Greg said, feeling glad that the inspector had heard the raving lunatic for himself. "Now you know what kind of maniac we're up against. We locked him in a jail cell."

"Anybody else there, besides you and your girlfriend?" the inspector asked.

Greg smiled at the thought of Lisa being his girlfriend. Was she his girlfriend? Or just a friend? He hadn't thought about it before—even though he had already told her he loved her. Did he mean it, or had he just said it because she had said it first? No, there was no question about it—he really loved her. "There's nobody else here now except me and my girlfriend, but there was a prisoner locked up in back yesterday. Sheriff Clifford was beating the heck out of him. We don't know what happened to him," Greg explained. "He's not in his cell today."

The inspector was silent for a moment. "Okay, son ... tell you what I'm going to do. I have no idea who you are or whether or not you're telling me the truth. You have to understand that it's not every day that I get a report about a giant catfish gobbling up people and dogs, and then a sheriff who allegedly goes berserk and attacks his prisoners. For all I know, you could be making this whole thing up, and that guy I hear ranting in the background could be just another prisoner. Or maybe it *is* the sheriff carrying on, in which case I would be very upset, too, if someone locked me up in my own jail!"

Greg started to protest, but the inspector cut him off.

"Let me finish, son. Let me finish. Okay, so what I'm going to do is drive up there first thing tomorrow morning from Madison. It's about a four-hour drive, so you can expect me there around ten o'clock. I'll meet you there at the sheriff's office."

Sheriff Clifford unleashed a new wave of obscenities from his jail cell in the rear of the building. He was screaming in specific detail what he would do to Greg and Lisa when he got his hands on them again.

Lisa shuddered, then folded her arms across her chest, hugging herself, and shaking her head in shocked disbelief. She glanced at Greg, a look of urgency on her face. "We gotta get out of here," she said gravely.

Greg nodded and held up his index finger, indicating to her that they would be leaving in just a second.

"Meanwhile," the inspector went on, "since Pine Acres is the closest town to Wolverine, I'm going to call Sheriff Willoughby in Pine Acres and ask him to send one of his deputies over to Wolverine to babysit Sheriff Clifford until I get there tomorrow."

"Okay," Greg said, "but I'm taking the jail keys with me. I'm not taking any chances of someone letting that maniac out of jail before you get here." His stomach churned and somersaulted at the thought of Sheriff Clifford being free and attacking Lisa again.

"That's fine, son," Inspector Gramms replied. "If you're telling me the truth, I wouldn't want him out, either." He paused, then continued. "And if you *are* telling me the truth, then that means you and your girlfriend are not criminals, in which case you won't be needing Sheriff Clifford's gun. So I want you to leave it in a desk drawer or somewhere out of sight, so no one else comes along and picks it up. Understand?"

Greg eyed the .357 magnum on the desk where Lisa had set it. He was reluctant to leave the gun behind, but he realized the inspector was right—there really was no need for him or Lisa to carry it around with them. After all, the sheriff was safely locked up, and *they* had the keys. "Okay," he said. "No problem. I'll leave it in the top left drawer of his desk."

When Greg hung up, he felt ecstatic that help was on the way. He related the conversation to Lisa. "Now we're getting somewhere," he said, relieved.

"But Inspector Gramms won't be here until tomorrow at ten o'clock," Lisa said, worried. She was still hugging herself, obviously still upset. "What'll we do in the meantime?"

Sheriff Clifford was still screaming from his cell in the rear of the building. "LET ME OUT OF HERE! DO YOU HEAR ME! I'LL KILL YOU! LET ME OUT!"

Greg stood up from the desk, went to Lisa, and slipped his arm around her waist. "What we do now is get out of here," he said, escorting her out the front door.

"Where to?"

"We'll hike to your cabin first so you can pick up some more clothes and stuff. Then we can drive your speedboat over to *my* cabin so I can pick up some more things for me and Jenny and the twins. Then we'll take your boat over to the Tuckers'. We can spend the night there again. Okay?"

"But my cabin is ten miles away," Lisa protested. "Couldn't we just call Mr. Tucker and have him come out here and pick us up?"

"No way," Greg said matter-of-factly. He held her hand as they descended the steps in front of the sheriff's office. He was headed for the sand road at the edge of town that would take them back to Mink Lake.

"Why not?"

"Because there's no phone on Tucker Island. Remember? And even if there was, Mr. Tucker's speedboat is now at the bottom of the lake—thanks to the giant catfish that he insists doesn't exist!"

"So they're all stranded on Tucker Island until we arrive with *my* boat."

"That's right," he said, "unless they use my rowboat that I left there."

Lisa let her head droop in despair. "But, Greg ... it's ten miles! Couldn't we ask someone in town to give us a ride to my place?"

"No," Greg said, shaking his head. "Too many people saw us handcuffed in the back seat of Sheriff Clifford's patrol car when he brought us in this morning. They know that something's up with us, and they might get suspicious if we walk around town, asking people for a ride."

"Suspicious of what? We haven't done anything wrong. You make us sound like a couple of criminals!"

Greg rolled his eyes. "Look, *I* know we're not criminals, and *you* know we're not criminals, but if we can't convince the sheriff or the Tuckers of our story, how are we going to convince the townsfolk?"

"We don't have to convince them of anything," Lisa argued. "We'll simply ask them for a ride to my place, and on the way there, we won't tell them a single, solitary thing. Simple!"

Greg shook his head. "It's *not* that simple. For all we know, Sheriff Clifford may have a lot of loyal friends around here. And people are nosy—especially in a small town like this. They'll ask questions, all right. They'll wanna know what's up with us and the sheriff. Then they might get offended when we try to dodge their questions. One thing could lead to the next." He rubbed his free hand over his flattop. "Who knows how they'll react, what they might do. I don't want anymore trouble. Let's just get outa here, go home, and wait for Inspector Gramms. So we walk for a while—it's not a big deal."

Lisa sighed, shrugged her shoulders, and continued to hold his hand as they walked. "I hope we can at least get back before dark."

It was late afternoon, and Greg reasoned there should be enough time to cover the ten miles before dark. But an uneasiness fell over him when he noticed an ugly black and blue sky in the south. But the sun was still shining in the west. We'll be all right, he thought, trying to convince himself. But the feeling of gloom still hung over him like the bruised sky above.

* * *

About an hour later, Lisa complained that her feet were tired and sore. "You think we're halfway there yet?" she asked, stopping at the edge of the road. She plopped down on the foot-high sandy berm that shouldered the road on both sides and massaged her ankles.

"No ... I think we're maybe a third of the way," Greg said, his eyes scanning the endless stretch of sandy road before him. A wall of pine trees bordered the road on both sides. "It's probably only a couple of hours before we reach your cabin." He turned and looked in the direction from which they had just come, noting the miles of sand road they had already covered. "I can't believe we've come this far already." He drew the back of his hand across his forehead, wiping away beads of perspiration. "We're making pretty good time." Suddenly his eye caught a puff of dust in the road, far off in the distance. "Looks like a car coming."

"Where?" Lisa cried, jumping up, straining her eyes in the direction Greg was pointing. "Maybe we can hitch a ride!" she said, excited.

The idea of getting a ride excited Greg, too. He was hot, tired, and thirsty. A ride right about now would be a Godsend. But as the dust cloud drew closer, his excitement quickly dampened. Even at that great distance, he could make out the outline of two small nubs protruding from the top of the car. "It's a police car!" he cried, his heart racing.

"How can you tel—"

Greg interrupted her by grabbing her hand, jumping over the sand berm, then charging into the underbrush, dodging pine trees and scrub oaks. When they were perhaps thirty yards into the forest, he stopped and crouched behind some bushes, pulling Lisa down beside him.

"Are you nuts or something!" she asked, annoyed. "What are you—"

"Quiet!" he snapped, peering cautiously over the top of the thicket. "Here it comes!"

The car rumbled by in a cloud of sand. The pair of emergency lights jutting from the top were unmistakable, as was the dark scowling face of Sheriff Clifford, clenching a cigar in his teeth, his wild eyes bulging from their sockets.

Lisa gasped, obviously shocked at the sight of the maniac sheriff. "How'd he get out of jail?" she asked, standing up, now that the car had safely passed.

Greg stood and brushed pine needles and bits of leaves from his jeans. "The deputy sheriff from Pine Acres probably let him out with an extra set of keys that were tucked away somewhere in the office."

Now that the car had passed, his heartbeat was beginning to return to normal. "Thank God he didn't see us."

"What'll we do now?" she asked, folding her arms across her chest, hugging herself.

He didn't have a clue as to what to do next, but he didn't want her to know it. *She's upset enough the way it is,* he thought, putting his arm around her, hugging her. *It's my fault she's mixed up in this mess. Have to protect her the best I can.* "We can't go home now," he said, fumbling for a plan. "Sheriff Clifford will be waiting for us—at your cabin, or my cabin, or the Tuckers'." Greg chewed on his lip, thinking. "We'll just have to hide in the woods until tomorrow morning, when Inspector Gramms arrives." He felt Lisa stiffen beside him, her eyes locked on his.

"Spend the night in the woods?" she asked incredulously. "What are you ... nuts?"

"You got a better idea?" he asked, feeling a little annoyed himself.

"You bet I do. We go straight to *my* cabin, pick up some clothes and things for me. Then we take my speedboat and go over to *your* cabin and pick up some more clothes for you and Jenny and the twins, then head straight for the Tuckers', where we spend the night again. Tomorrow morning, we go back to my cabin, pick up my car, and drive straight to the sheriff's office, where we meet Inspector Gramms." She broke away from him, facing him. "Understand?"

Now Greg stared incredulously at *her*. "That's the same exact plan we had to begin with."

"I know," she said, walking away from him. "It's a good plan, and we're sticking to it."

Greg rolled his eyes. "Where are you going?"

"Back to the road." She stopped and turned to face him. "You coming?"

He chuckled, shaking his head. "You may be good with cars, but your sense of direction is worthless. The road is over there," he said, pointing in the opposite direction in which she was headed.

"No, it's not. It's this way. I can see it from here." She walked a few more yards, sidestepping tree trunks, pushing her way through the underbrush.

Greg called after her, straining to see her through the woods. "Lisa, come back. You're going the wrong way. The road is this way. Trust me."

"Don't be silly, Greg," she answered. "I'm standing on the road right now. Come here and see for yourself."

Puzzled, Greg followed her short trail through the brush until it gave way to another sandy road. Standing beside her, he examined the road carefully. "This isn't the main road," he said, taking note that this road was much narrower than the main road. Tall weeds lined both edges of this lesser road, arching over and spilling onto the roadway itself. Interwoven pine boughs formed a dark canopy above. Every few feet, branches were jutting out from both sides, making a partial barricade. "There's barely room for a car to squeeze through," Greg said. He pointed to the ground. "And look, there aren't any tire tracks at all."

"It looks like this road hasn't been used for quite some time," Lisa said. Then she pointed to a pile of dead brush some fifty feet away. "What's that?"

Greg said, "Let's check it out."

The brush pile was six feet high and completely blocked the road. Just on the other side of the pile was the main road—the road they had originally been walking on when Sheriff Clifford had zoomed by.

"Looks like somebody deliberately stacked this brush pile here to hide this road," Greg said. "But why?"

Lisa put her hands on her hips, her brow furrowed, scanning the dark, scrubby road ahead. "I wonder where it goes?"

"Come on," Greg said, grabbing her hand. "Only one way to find out."

The road meandered through the woods for half a mile, twisting and turning every few yards beneath the canopy of pine, oak, maple, and aspen branches. It ended in a vast clearing that was peppered with stumps of all kinds and sizes.

"This must be an old logging trail," Greg said. "Probably hasn't been used for years."

Lisa stooped to pick something up off the ground. "Well, somebody's been here a lot more recently than that," she said, holding up a faded, but intact, cigar butt.

While Greg examined the cigar butt, Lisa said, "Hey, look ... another brush pile."

Huddled in the far corner of the clearing was an enormous pile of dead brush. Even though Greg had determined that this was an old logging site, and that a huge pile of dead brush might well be expected to be found in such an area, there was something mysterious about this brush pile—something out of place. Portions of *this* brush pile were glittering in the fading sunlight.

His curiosity peaked, Greg ran over to the pile to investigate. "Well, I'll be darned," he said, pulling off a couple of dead branches from the pile.

"What is it?" Lisa asked, running up behind him.

Greg couldn't believe what he was seeing. He pulled another dead branch from the pile, revealing more of the object that he stood gaping at.

Hidden beneath the pile of dead branches, twigs, leaves, and slabs of bark was a car—a two-door Ford. Obviously someone had gone to great length to camouflage it, for it had been sprayed with black, brown, and green paint. Here and there, a few spots of chrome bumper and chrome trim had been missed, allowing sunlight to glitter upon the smooth, shiny surfaces. Greg removed enough branches to allow him to open the driver's door.

"It's unlocked," he said, sliding behind the steering wheel.

Apparently the car had at one time been white in color, for the edge of the door had been spared the dappled spray paint as well.

Greg noticed the dome light flickered on when he opened the car door.

"I don't think this car has been here that long," he said.

"No, it couldn't have been because the battery is still good," Lisa said, poking her head inside the car. "Why would anyone go to all this trouble to hide a car?"

And then it hit both of them at that moment, like a ton of bricks. They stared at each other for a split second, shocked.

"Rachel!" they cried in unison.

"Oh, my God, Greg! Could it be?" She scrambled to the front of the car, kneeled down, and began poking and pulling at the brush pile. Then she scurried to the rear of the car and did the same thing. A moment later, she came back to the driver's side and informed Greg that there were no plates on the car.

Greg leaned over in the driver's seat and opened the glove compartment. "Empty." He turned around and kneeled on the front seat, his eyes scanning the floor and the seat in back. "Nothing." He slid out of the car, leaned across the front seat, and searched for anything that might have been left there. "Nothing under there, either." He stood up with his hands on his hips, staring at the car, chewing his lower lip. "It's clean. Completely clean."

"Let's check the trunk," Lisa said.

"We can't. We don't have the keys."

Lisa smiled confidently. "We don't need the keys," she said, leaning inside the car and pulling the front seat forward. Then she climbed in the back and began pulling the rear seat out.

Greg was dumbfounded. "Are you sure?"

"Yes, I'm sure. You said it yourself—I know my cars. Now don't just stand there—give me a hand."

Moments later they removed the back seat, and Greg lay on his stomach and crawled into the trunk.

"Anything?" Lisa asked hopefully.

"Not yet," he replied, groping with his fingers in the semidarkness. He squirmed farther back into the trunk, running his fingers along the seam on all three sides where the walls and floor intersected.

"Anything?" Lisa asked again, her tone desperate.

"No, there's nothing he—" His fingers touched something lying on the floor against the back wall. It was something thin, metallic. He grasped the object in his hand and backed out of the trunk. "I got something!"

"What is it?" Lisa asked, excited. She huddled close to Greg, as he climbed out of the car.

He held up his hand, letting the object dangle from his fingertips. It was a necklace, a gold necklace with a gold, heart-shaped charm. "There's an inscription on the back," Greg said, holding the piece close to his face. "It says, 'TO RACHEL WITH LOVE ... FROM GRANDMA AND GRANDPA.'" Greg stared in shock at Lisa. A cold chill ran up his spine, causing the hairs on his neck to stand on end.

CHAPTER 8

Greg got the idea of driving Rachel's car out of the woods and back to Lisa's cabin, in order to save them the time and trouble of walking. "That is ...if you know how to hot-wire it," he said.

"Trust me," Lisa said confidently. "That's no problem for me. But first we'd better make sure the car hasn't been disabled, before we go through the trouble of removing *all* of the brush pile from around it." After popping the hood, she quickly determined that the car had, indeed, been disabled. "The distributor cap is missing," she said matter-of-factly.

"That figures. So whoever dumped the car here wanted to make sure it *stayed* here."

"Yeah, and I think we have a pretty good idea of who that someone is," Lisa said, closing the hood. "Well ... let's put this rear seat back into place and be on our way."

"Okay," Greg agreed. "And we'd better put back the brush we've already removed. I think it's best to keep this car completely hidden until we can show it to Inspector Gramms tomorrow morning. I don't want anyone to find it or mess around with it before then."

Having replaced the brush around the car, Greg and Lisa hiked the rest of the way to Lisa's cabin. As they walked up the driveway, Greg noticed the hood was up on her parked Mustang.

Lisa peered under the hood, then straightened up, clutching a black plastic cylinder with several dangling wires. The cylinder was cracked and the wires were all cut clean. "Guess who?" she said sarcastically.

"Sheriff Clifford strikes again?"

"Yep!" She tossed the debris on the ground, obviously infuriated. "How dare that maniac mess with my car! I can't believe he actually tore out my distributor cap!"

Greg felt the tiny hairs stand up on the back of his neck again. The thought of Sheriff Clifford trying to prevent their escape made his stomach somersault and his knees tremble. "He's a psychopath!"

Lisa slammed the hood shut. "What about the boats— my speedboat and the dead fisherman's boat?"

Greg looked at her, surprised. He had forgotten about the two boats. "Good question!" He dashed past Lisa's cabin, down the hill, and out onto her dock.

The fisherman's aluminum boat was still tied to the side of the dock where they had left it earlier that morning, but it wasn't *exactly* the way they had left it. The boat now lay at the bottom of the lake in three feet of water.

Even in the fading daylight, Greg could see three gaping holes where bullets had pierced the aluminum bottom.

Lisa joined him on the dock, eyeing the sunken craft. "That maniac actually shot the boat?"

"He sure did," Greg replied, shaking his head in disgust.

"Oh, great! I can't wait to see what he did to my speedboat," Lisa said, marching to the end of the dock where it was tied.

Greg followed her and watched as she stepped down into her boat and began checking the wiring under the control console. "Anything?" he asked.

"The wiring looks okay," she said, turning the key in the ignition.

But nothing happened—the engine was completely dead.

Lisa removed the rear seat and the cushioned backrest above it, exposing the motor and battery compartment. "He took the battery!" Stunned, she stepped out of the boat and stood on the dock, facing Greg. "Now what'll we do? We can't go anywhere—we don't have a car or a boat!"

"And we can't stay here," Greg added. "He could come back at any time and we'd be sitting ducks."

"Greg, I don't like this," she said, her voice cracking. "I'm scared." She ran a hand through her red tousled hair and sighed, trying to regain her composure. Tears were welling in her brown eyes.

Greg put his arm around her, held her. He could feel her taking a deep breath. "It's okay, Lisa. It's okay to be scared. I'm scared, too."

"I can't believe this is happening." She laid her head on his shoulder. "It seems like I've spent my whole life being scared of something." She slipped her arms around his waist, hugging him. "Scared of not being loved by my parents—especially since their divorce. Scared of not getting good grades in school. Scared of not having any friends." She looked up at him, gazing in his eyes. "Real friends." She hugged him tighter. "Scared of not having a successful career. Scared of not finding a loving husband and having kids someday." She pondered a moment. "Scared of ... of life, I guess." She fell silent momentarily, staring down at her dirty sneakers.

A few yards away on the shore, a whippoorwill flitted

and fluttered in a birch tree. It perched on a small branch and whistled. Its loud, sharp song pierced the evening stillness over and over again, like a broken record. WHIP-POOR-WILL! WHIP-POOR-WILL! WHIP-POOR-WILL! WHIP-POOR-WILL!

She looked up at him again, her eyes searching his. "Do you know what I mean?"

"Yeah, I think I do," Greg lied. Actually, he didn't really understand what she meant at all. He couldn't relate to being scared all of the time—or at all—for until this vacation started just a few days ago, he had never known fear—real fear—before. And he was totally surprised to hear that *she* of all people was scared of life, for she had—for the most part—portrayed herself as being tough, confident, spunky, and cocky. Was it all just an act? And if so, perhaps there were a lot of people in the world who were merely "acting." He felt awkward, bewildered, for he had never had a deep conversation with anyone like this before. It was kind of weird. And yet he felt for her, and he was trying to understand, trying to be her friend—a real friend. Feeling uncomfortable, he wasn't sure of what to do next, what to say next. "I guess I've always been worried that I wouldn't measure up to my dad's standards."

She looked at him, puzzled. "Your dad?"

He felt a little stupid, embarrassed. He had never confessed anything like that to anyone else before. Would she think lesser of him now? Was he a weakling in her eyes now? A wimp? Perhaps he was revealing too much of himself. Perhaps he shouldn't have said anything. Perhaps he should just shut up now. Perhaps ... but he couldn't. Suddenly he didn't want to shut up. In fact, it was beginning to feel good to bare one's soul to another human being, to someone he could ... trust? "My dad is one of those big, strong, macho types—always bossing me around, criticizing every move I make. You know ... never measuring up in his eyes. He makes me feel stupid, inadequate, and ... angry."

"Do you love him?" Lisa asked, with sincere interest.

The question caught Greg totally by surprise. He'd never thought about his dad that way. *Did* he love him? He didn't know if he loved his dad or not. "Well, I don't think I *hate* him."

"So you love him, right?"

"Well, sometimes I get so mad at him, I wish I could kick his butt. And sometimes I wish my mom would throw him out and get a divorce." Wow! Where did *that* come from? he thought. Had he become a hateful monster—a by-product of his dismal childhood? Was he being disloyal? He felt a twinge of guilt.

"But do you love him?" she persisted.

He thought of all the confrontations he had had with his dad lately. Then he looked her in the eye. "I honestly don't know."

"Aren't you scared?" she asked.

"Of what?"

"Of the fact that your dad might feel the same way about you—not love you?"

Greg pursed his lips, thinking. The thought of Dad not loving him *did* bother him—much to his surprise. All this talk about him and Dad loving each other was beginning to make him feel uncomfortable. How'd they get on the subject, anyhow? "I've never done anything to cause my dad *not* to love me."

"But—"

Lisa was cut off by a low rumbling noise that reverberated around the lake.

"Sounds like thunder," Greg said, grabbing her hand. "Come on, we'd better get going."

"Where to?"

"Back to Rachel's car. We can spend the night there, then walk into town tomorrow morning to meet Inspector Gramms."

"But it's almost dark," she protested.

"Yeah, and it looks like rain, so let's get moving. There's no time to waste." He led her off the dock and back up the hill to her cabin.

Lightning ripped the sky and thunder rattled the earth.

"Are you sure we can't just stay here?" Lisa pleaded.

"No, we can't stay here because sooner or later that maniac of a sheriff will be back, looking for us. And my cabin won't be any safer. And since we don't have a boat to get to Tucker Island, I say we spend the night in Rachel's car. At least we'll be safe there until morning."

"Okay, you're right. But give me a minute to gather some things in my overnight bag," she said, dashing into her cabin.

Another clap of thunder shook the ground, causing the whippoorwill to stop his whistle in mid-song and flutter away.

"Hurry up!" he called after her.

* * *

Later, after trudging over miles of sand road, Greg and Lisa arrived at the old logging road that would lead them to the abandoned car. It was completely dark now, and Greg felt the first drop of rain. Lightning flashed in the sky every now and then, stabbing the horizon, casting intermittent light on the trail ahead. Eerie shadows loomed ominously in the flickering light, then shuddered under crashing thunder. The rain began to pelt the forest relentlessly, drowning out all other sounds of the wilderness.

Greg led the way, carefully picking his way through branches that jutted out over the narrow roadway. He was leery of poking an eye on the protruding twigs. He was soaking wet now, but at least it was still warm outside, having been a particularly hot and muggy day. The thick treetop canopy offered little protection from the pounding rain.

He knew Lisa must be feeling every bit as miserable as he was. But at least she isn't complaining about it, he thought, grateful for that.

He imagined what it would be like if he were out here right now with his sister, Jenny, instead of with Lisa. Jenny's constant whining and sniveling would only make matters worse—for both of them.

He was beginning to realize that Lisa wasn't like a lot of other girls might be. She was different somehow. Tough, but at the same time ...tender. Strong, but ... vulnerable. Independent, but ...dependent.

I like it, he thought, smiling to himself. She's ...special. Very, very special. He switched her lavender overnight bag that he was carrying for her to his left hand, then grabbed her hand with his right. He gave it a squeeze, and he felt her squeeze back.

Ten minutes later, they trudged up to Rachel's car, wet and weary.

Greg removed a clump of wet brush—just enough for them to open the driver's door and crawl inside. Greg followed Lisa into the back seat and set the drenched overnight bag on the front seat. Then he pulled the door shut behind him.

Outside, rain plunked down on the roof of the car, making Greg feel safe and cozy inside. Perhaps too cozy. "It's hot and stuffy in here," he said, rolling down the driver's window and then the passenger door window, about an inch each. "That should help circulate some air without letting in too much rain."

"Perfect," Lisa said.

In the darkness, he could make out her silhouette beside him. She leaned forward and shook her head, flicking rainwater from her hair.

Specks of rainwater landed on his face, and he put his hands up, feigning self-defense. "Hey, you do that as well as Spook," he said, chuckling.

"Spook? Oh, yeah ... your dog." She brought her legs up to her chest, wrapping her arms around them, resting her chin on her knees. "I'm really sorry about your dog."

Greg became solemn, thinking of Spook. "Thanks."

"At least he didn't suffer."

He felt his eyes misting and blinked hard. "No, he didn't suffer ... that's for sure."

She turned suddenly and faced him. "What's going on here, Greg?" she blurted. "I mean ... first there's the monster catfish swallowing everyone, then there's the sheriff who arrests us because he thinks we murdered that fisherman, then the sheriff attacks me, and then we find Rachel's car—at least it appears to be her car—abandoned and camouflaged in the woods." She sighed, running her hand through her hair. "It's like everything bad is happening all at once."

"It's like a nightmare," Greg agreed. "If this is Rachel's car, then what in the world happened to Rachel? She's been missing since last year."

"Most likely she's dead," Lisa said sadly. "Poor Rachel."

"Poor Mr. and Mrs. Tucker," Greg added. "How are we going to tell them that we think we found her car and that she's probably dead?"

"Maybe Inspector Gramms will know best how to tell them. We'll bring him here tomorrow morning to show him the car. He'll know what to do."

"You think that cigar butt we found here belongs to Sheriff Clifford?"

"Could be," Lisa answered, "but then again, lots of people smoke cigars. It might belong to a logger, a hunter, or a trapper. We just don't know."

"You think Sheriff Clifford had anything to do with Rachel's disappearance?"

"Well, being that he's a maniac, I'd be surprised if he didn't."

"But he's a sheriff, for pete's sake! He's supposed to be helping people, protecting people, not harming them!" Greg recalled the attack on Lisa back in the jail cell, and his blood began to boil all over again. He fisted his hands, just thinking about it.

"He's a mad dog with a gun and a badge," Lisa corrected him. "Completely insane—if you ask me."

Greg thought about the gun. The more he thought about it, the more he wished he had ignored Inspector Gramms' advice to leave the .357 magnum behind. That gun would come in real handy right about now, he thought. Just in case.

A bolt of lightning ripped the sky, illuminating the rain-drenched forest surrounding them. An instant later, an earsplitting clap of thunder exploded outside, rattling the car.

Lisa shuddered. "That reminds me—I've gotta get out of these wet clothes. Would you mind handing me my overnight bag?"

Greg reached over into the front seat, grabbed the bag, and handed it to her. "The bag is drenched, so everything inside is probably wet, too."

Lisa smiled as she unzipped the bag. "Don't worry," she said, opening a plastic garbage liner, "I've already thought of that. That's why I put all my things inside this garbage bag first." She removed some clothing from the bag.

"Everything's nice and dry. And now if you don't mind, please climb into the front seat and keep your eyes straight ahead—no peeking!"

Greg obliged her, and after she had changed into her dry clothes, she asked, "What time did you say we're meeting Inspector Gramms tomorrow?"

"Ten o'clock."

"Then it's time to turn in."

Greg started to move toward the back seat, but Lisa stopped him by holding up her hand.

"You're fine right where you are," she said nonchalantly.

"But I—"

"Good night, Greg. Sweet dreams." Using her overnight bag as a pillow, she lied down on the back seat in a fetal position and closed her eyes.

Greg stretched out on the front seat and stared at the car's ceiling. "Good night," he said, then closed his eyes and fell asleep.

* * *

Hours later, the sharp banging of car doors slamming shut jarred Greg awake.

"What's that?" he whispered, raising his head off the seat.

He heard Lisa stir in the back seat. "What time is i—?"

"Shh!" Greg whispered. "Somebody's here!" Hearing voices outside, he slowly peered over the dashboard. His heart sank at the sight before him, making him sick to his stomach. "Lisa, stay down! Don't move!"

Parked fifty feet away in the old logging clearing was Sheriff Clifford's patrol car. Parked directly behind it was a tan, four-door Plymouth. Even if Greg had not noticed the chrome spotlight mounted on the driver's door, or the long steel antenna that was arched from the trunk lid to the rear fender, he couldn't have possibly missed the bright blue and gold emblem on the driver's door, with the words "STATE POLICE" printed in a semicircle above.

Standing next to the state police patrol car were Sheriff Clifford and a middle-aged man in a suit and tie. They appeared to be engaged in an intense conversation.

Greg strained to hear what they were saying.

"I found the body lying right over there," Sheriff Clifford said, pointing past the police cars. "The way I figure it, the boyfriend drove her out here under false pretenses, then killed her. I can only assume that jealousy was the motive."

Greg kept his head down and watched the two men carefully. That must be Inspector Gramms, he thought. But what if it isn't? Should I call out to him, or stay in hiding?

"Where was the body exactly?" the man in the suit and tie asked. He was walking ahead of Sheriff Clifford, his hands thrust inside his pockets, studying the ground.

"Right about where you're standing," Sheriff Clifford said, raising his .357 magnum and pointing it at the back of the man's head.

Horrified, Greg clenched his eyes shut and ducked behind the dashboard, just as the gun went off.

BOOM!

CHAPTER 9

There was a moment of dead silence after the gun had roared. Greg froze, straining to hear, his heart hammering. After a few moments, he heard someone moving about. Then he heard the familiar sound of a trunk lid popping open. Finally curiosity got the better of him, and he slowly raised his head high enough to peer over the dashboard. He looked just in time to see the suit and tie man's legs and feet disappear into the trunk of Sheriff Clifford's patrol car.

Apparently Lisa saw it, too. "Oh, my God, Greg! He just put a body in his trunk!" Her head was up just high enough to see above the top of the front seat.

"Shh!" Greg whispered. "Keep your head down and don't move!"

"Oh, Greg! I'm so scared!" she said in a harsh whisper. "We're going to die! We're going to die, Greg! What'll we do?" she whimpered.

"Be quiet! He doesn't know we're here. Don't move! We'll be okay as long as we stay quiet and he doesn't see us." He tried to make himself sound convincing, believable, but that was very hard to do, since he, himself, had come unglued, shaking uncontrollably. Suddenly a new fear ripped through his mind, churning his gut: What if Sheriff Clifford noticed that some of the brush had been removed from the car they were hiding in? What if he noticed the windows had been opened an inch or so? No doubt Sheriff Clifford would then approach the car and find them hiding inside. Then what? After what he and Lisa had just witnessed, the answer was clear—*they* would be next! Terrified, his heart was banging frantically, his blood surging in his temples. Suddenly he heard Sheriff Clifford outside, talking to himself.

"So Mr. Hotshot State Police Inspector, looks like your inspecting days are over. Looks like you're not so much after all. Heh, heh, heh."

Curious, Greg slowly raised his head again and peered over the dashboard, watching Sheriff Clifford as he stood at the rear of his patrol car, the trunk lid still open, talking to the corpse inside.

"You're nothing but fish food, Inspector Gramms. Nothing but glorified fish food. Heh, heh, heh. I wonder if ole Whiskers will like cop meat. But don't you worry Inspector—of all the people I've fed him, he ain't never turned down a one of them. Heh, heh, heh. Of course, most of them was young, pretty women. But every once in a while, I throw in a prisoner from skid row. Like I say, ole Whiskers doesn't turn down anybody. Fish food is fish food. Heh, heh, heh."

Suddenly the police radio inside Inspector Gramms' car began to hiss and cackle. Seconds later, a female voice erupted through the static.

"Attention Wasp Nine. Attention Wasp Nine. Please state your ten-twenty."

Sheriff Clifford slammed the trunk lid shut, then swaggered over to the state police car. With a beefy hand, he withdrew his .357 magnum from its holster, pointed it through the open window and said, "Here's your ten-twenty, sweetheart!"

The roar of the gun shattered the morning stillness once more, as well as the radio, the blast thundering through the woods.

Then ... silence.

"Oh, God, Greg!" Lisa whimpered. "What's he doing now?"

"Shh! Don't make a sound," he whispered. He continued to watch the sheriff.

Sheriff Clifford went back to his patrol car, removed several cans of spray paint from beneath the front seat, then proceeded to spray the state police car. First, using black paint, he made long horizontal lines along the length of the car on both sides and on top. Next, using brown paint, he began spraying between the original lines. Finally, he removed the plastic cap from another can of paint, then shook the can. The steel ball bearing inside the can made a rattling sound as he shook it.

SSSSSSSSSSSSSSSSSSSSSSSSSSSSSSSSSSSSSSSSSSSSSSSSSSS!

The sheriff sprayed green paint all over the car in squiggly, vertical lines.

A short while later, Inspector Gramms' car was completely camouflaged with spray paint.

As a final touch, Sheriff Clifford began covering the car with dead branches, ferns, and slabs of dead bark. As he covered the car, he began talking out loud again to the corpse.

"It's a good thing you came along when you did, Inspector. Ole Whiskers was getting mighty hungry out there in Mink Lake. Starting to attack people left and right. That's because I ain't fed him any pretty young women lately. Heh, heh, heh. Of course I *did* feed him an alcoholic vagrant the other day. But heck, that fella was so skinny he couldn't satisfy a sparrow."

Apparently Sheriff Clifford noticed a patch of chrome bumper glinting in the sunlight through the quilted maze of branches. He opened the can of green paint again, shook it, rattling it, then sprayed the chrome area through openings in the dead brush.

SSSSSSSSSSSSSSSSSSSSSSSSSSSSSSSSSSSS!

Then the sheriff jabbed a cigar into his mouth, lit it, then swaggered around the car, puffing on his cigar, examining his handiwork. "You see, Inspector," he said smugly, "ole Whiskers is a mutant—a freak—an accident of the radiation leak from the Pine Acres nuclear power plant. First, the Wolverine River was contaminated, and because the river runs through Mink Lake, it didn't take long to contaminate everything in the lake, as well. And ole Whiskers—well heck—he's just a freak of nature, a victim of the nuclear fallout. Before the radiation leak, he was just your average catfish, swimming around, minding his own business. But after the accident, he began to grow. And grow. And grow! Heh, heh, heh."

The sheriff removed the cigar from his mouth, sucked up an enormous wad of phlegm and cigar juice and spit it on the ground. Then he continued.

"When I first seen 'im, I couldn't believe my eyes. And then I got to thinkin'—that big ole catfish is gotta have some kinda appetite. And since I get all these bodies now and then from my extracurricular activities, I figure, heck, I might as well feed 'em to ole Whiskers. After all, somebody's got to keep 'im fed. Or else he'll just go off on a rampage—like he done here this week—eating up everyone and everything in sight. Now you know, Inspector, that sooner or later somebody would start complaining about a giant, man-eating catfish. Then word would get around, and before ya know it, every jackass and his brother from all over the country would be out here, prying and probing, trying to get a shot at the monster—like they did with that monster shark in *Jaws.*"

He took a long drag on his cigar, then let the smoke escape through his flared nostrils. "So I figure, heck, I can't let 'em take away my natural garbage disposal system. Heh, heh, heh. I mean, what the heck am I supposed to do then … start burying my bodies?" He sucked the air through his nose and throat, and spit out another huge wad. "That's why I'm glad you come along when you did, Gramms. Tonight I'll dump your body in the lake for ole Whiskers, and nobody will ever know you was here."

He squinted in the bluegray cigar smoke swirling around his head. "Then I have to get me them two kids—Lisa and her pal, whatever his name is. They'll be a real pleasure to kill. And what the heck—it'll be more fish food for ole Whiskers. Heh, heh, heh. That oughta satisfy his appetite, keep 'im quiet for a while."

The sheriff swaggered back to his patrol car, opened the door, then paused. Resting his elbows between the top of the car and the top of the driver's door, he removed the cigar from his mouth and flicked it onto the ground. "Yep …ole Whiskers is gonna eat like a king again. Bon appetite!" He got in his car, turned it around in the clearing, then slowly drove away.

When the sheriff's car was no longer visible around a bend in the old logging trail, Greg sat upright and turned toward Lisa. "He's gone!"

Lisa sprang up from the rear seat, her eyes wide with terror.

Greg stared in shock at her, taking deep breaths to calm his own nerves. Finally, opening the car door, he said, "We gotta get outa here!"

He didn't have to repeat himself, for Lisa was clinging to him, tighter than ever, her face ashen.

"Greg, I think I'm going to throw up," she said, her voice

trembling, her eyes watering. She let go of Greg and put one hand over her mouth and clutched her stomach with the other.

"Take some deep breaths," Greg said. "It's probably just nerves." He was worried about her, felt bad for her, and his concern for her made him forget about his own fear—for the time being.

After taking a few deep breaths, Lisa sat down on a log and bent her head between her legs. "I feel a little dizzy now."

Greg sat down beside her, placing his arm around her shoulders, holding her. "I'm so sorry I let you get mixed up in this mess. Had I known how dangerous all of this was going to turn out, I would've never let you get involved."

She brought her head up, smiled weakly. "I know, but it's not your fault. I *insisted* on tagging along, and neither one of us could've known the evil that lay ahead of us." She put her hand on his leg. "Besides, at least I got to meet you." She kissed him lightly on his mouth. "To love you."

He smiled warmly at her. "Thanks. I love you, too. Feeling better?"

She took a deep breath, then exhaled. "Much better." Suddenly she jumped to her feet, her eyes wide with alarm once more. "Where do we go from here? I mean, now that we know that Sheriff Clifford probably murdered the Tuckers' granddaughter, Rachel, and Inspector Gramms, where do we go? What'll we do?"

Greg didn't hesitate a moment. He sprang up and faced her, determined. "We fight back—that's what we do!"

"Fight back? How?"

"We just heard Sheriff Clifford say he was looking for us, wanted to kill us and feed us to Whiskers. That means he's going to be out searching for us, and he might go looking at the Tuckers'. We have to get back to Tucker Island and warn them to steer clear of Sheriff Clifford. Maybe Mr. Tucker will know someone who we can call to help us—someone we can trust."

"But we don't have a boat to get to Tucker Island—remember? That maniac sheriff disabled my speedboat and the dead fisherman's boat."

Greg chewed his bottom lip, thinking. "Then we'll have to *steal* a boat—just temporarily. Can you hot-wire a speedboat?"

"No problem."

"Good. Once we get to Tucker Island, we can arm ourselves with some of Mr. Tucker's guns. You can stay with the Tuckers and Jenny and the twins. You'll be safer there. You and Mr. Tucker can arm yourselves and stand guard, just in case Sheriff Clifford shows up."

"Where will you be?"

"After I drop you off, I'll take the speedboat over to the public landing. Then I'll take Mr. Tucker's pickup truck and head out of town for help. I'll head south to Woodstream."

"But that's a hundred miles away," Lisa reminded him.

"Exactly! Far enough away that—hopefully—Sheriff Clifford won't have any buddies there. I wouldn't trust those deputies in Pine Acres. Apparently they're good pals with Sheriff Clifford. Being that they probably know him so well, and being that they're all police officers, they would never believe my story over Sheriff Clifford. Before you know it—he'd convince his cop buddies that *I've* been doing all the killing. I wouldn't stand a chance."

Lisa nodded her head in agreement. "Well ... let's go steal a boat."

Hiking back toward Mink Lake, they stopped at the first driveway that branched off the sand road.

"This one ought to lead us to a lakefront cabin," Greg said. "With any luck, they'll have a speedboat docked at their pier."

Strolling up the driveway, they paused when a brown clapboard-sided house came into view.

There was no one in sight, no movement, no noise.

Greg grabbed Lisa's hand, and the two of them crept past the house to the dock. As luck would have it, there *was* a speedboat tied to the pier.

Keeping an eye on the house, Greg said softly, "Okay, Lisa ... do your thing."

Lisa climbed inside the boat and within seconds she hot-wired the ignition and the motor sputtered to life.

Greg untied the boat's rope from the dock and hopped aboard. He glanced over his shoulder to see if anyone was coming, his adrenaline pumping.

Still no movement from the house. The coast was still clear.

Thank God, he thought. No one's home.

His nervous system began to unwind, as Lisa eased the throttle forward. "We'll stop at my cabin first," he said. "I have to get something before we go to Tucker Island."

Lisa nodded okay, then opened the throttle. The motor roared, and the boat shot away from the dock, zipping across the lake.

A short while later, they docked at Greg's pier and climbed the hill to his cabin. Inside, Greg stuffed a suitcase with more clothes and shoes for himself, Jenny, and the twins. Then he set it down in front of the door.

"What's that?" Lisa asked, pointing to the dented, five-gallon can next to the door.

"Oh, that's my dad's," Greg replied, removing two gallon jugs of milk from the refrigerator. He set one on the countertop, while emptying the other into the kitchen sink. "It's an obsolete pesticide called Chlordane. My dad was supposed to take it with him to the pest control convention in Pine Acres, but he forgot it."

Having emptied and rinsed out the first jug, he proceeded to empty the second one. "Chlordane is a very deadly pesticide—apparently so dangerous, the government banned its use anywhere in the United States. Except I guess you're allowed to use up whatever stock you might have on-hand. And that five gallons is what my dad had left over, and now he's trying to get rid of it by giving it away to some other exterminator."

When the second jug had been emptied into the sink, Greg knelt down, opened the cabinet door, and removed three more empty jugs that were stored under the sink. Dad had saved the jugs for adding water to his portable sprayer tanks. It was safer for Dad to fill the sprayer tanks from a jug, rather than placing the tanks in a sink to fill them. Greg placed all five of the empty jugs on the floor, lined up in a row. "But like I said, he forgot to bring it with him. And I'm glad he did."

"Why?"

Greg removed a package of bacon from the refrigerator, sliced it open with a kitchen knife, and peeled a few strips of bacon from the slab. Then he started rubbing the strips of bacon all over the outside of the jugs, smearing the greasy meat on the plastic containers. "Because I'm going to use this stuff to kill Whiskers. The AK-47 didn't even faze him. But if *this* stuff can't kill him, *nothing* will."

"Why the bacon?"

Rummaging in a cupboard above the sink, he found a plastic funnel and placed it in the top of the first jug. "Well, it's like you told me before, we have to entice the monster, make it come to us with the use of a scent. Like chumming for a shark. Like they did in that movie *Jaws.*"

Greg unscrewed the cap on the container of Chlordane and carefully poured the pesticide into the funnel, slowly filling the first jug.

"Very clever," Lisa said, beaming. "But do you think it will work?"

Greg continued pouring the deadly pesticide from the five-gallon can into each of the one-gallon plastic jugs. "Well, if you think about it, every time Whiskers attacked, there was always a strong scent of some kind associated with each of his victims. Like blood, or fish, or Spook—a doggy smell. And that ties in with the fact that catfish have a very good sense of smell. They can smell with their whiskers. In fact, that's how all catfish find their food—through their sense of smell." He capped each of the five jugs with the red plastic screw caps that originally came with each milk jug.

"So when Whiskers smells the bacon, he'll swallow the jugs of poison."

"Exactly."

"Greg, you're a genius!" Lisa cried, her face aglow. "I'm proud of you!"

"Thanks. But filling the jugs is the easy part. Feeding them to that monster is the hard part."

He opened a kitchen drawer, rummaged through it, then removed a pair of scissors. "I'll use these to pierce the jugs, just before I toss them to Whiskers. I wanna make sure the Chlordane is able to get out of the jugs and into the beast after he swallows them." He recalled Dad's stern warning about not dumping pesticides into a lake or any other body of water. "But I *don't* want the poison to escape into the lake." He slipped the scissors into his back pocket. "I don't wanna kill everything else in the lake."

"I understand," Lisa said, "but shouldn't you just let the authorities take care of Whiskers. Let them kill it. It's *their* problem—not yours."

"What are they gonna do—shoot it? We already know *that* doesn't work. And besides, Whiskers *is* my problem. He made it *personal* when he attacked me and you and Timmy and Spook. Don't worry, I'll alert the authorities in Woodstream about Sheriff Clifford. But I'm taking a crack at Whiskers myself." He held up a full jug in each hand. "And *this* time, I'll be ready for him."

Greg and Lisa loaded up the five jugs and the suitcase into the stolen speedboat, then whisked off across the lake toward Tucker Island.

A short while later, they were greeted at Tucker Island by Timmy and Tommy, who raced along the shoreline, wide-eyed and grinning, whooping and hollering, shouting Greg's name, then Lisa's, then Greg's again.

Greg smiled and waved at them as the boat approached the dock. Cute little guys, he thought. I'm lucky to have them for brothers.

Lisa let the boat glide alongside of the dock—what was left of it.

Greg secured the boat with a rope, helped Lisa out onto the dock, then stepped out himself. He kneeled down, and the twins came rushing into his open arms, still chanting his name.

"Gweg! Yea! Gweg is home! Yea! Gweg! Gweg!"

"Hey, you guys!" Greg said, chuckling. "How ya doing? Having fun?"

He rubbed their crew cut heads. "Are you guys being good for the Tuckers?"

"Yesssth!" they cried in perfect unison.

"Wh-wh-where you been, Gweg?" Tommy asked, poking his freckled nose in Greg's face. "We misssth you!"

"Yeah!" Timmy chimed in, throwing his arms around Greg's neck. "We misssth you!"

"Oh, yeah?" Greg said cheerily. "You did, huh? Well, guess what? I missed you, too!" He rubbed their fuzzy heads again. "So whaddaya think of that?" It was good to be back, good to see the twins again. He noticed Timmy was back to his old self—all happy and chipper again—and he was glad of that. Thank God the giant catfish attack on Timmy didn't leave any permanent scars—psychological *or* physical. Just scared the daylights out of him, Greg thought. Poor little guy. He gave the twins each another hug, then stood up to greet Jenny, who walked up to them, her brow furrowed.

She looked concerned, worried.

As Greg switched his attention to Jenny, the twins quickly switched theirs to Lisa, greeting her with the same level of excitement.

Jenny said, "Mr. Tucker is mad at you. He said you took his boat and his gun, and you never asked permission. Then you didn't even come home last night. He was afraid you and Lisa were stranded somewhere in that storm." Fingering her ponytail, she poked it into her mouth, her silvery braces chomping on the split ends.

Greg winced in disgust, then caught himself and smiled. "Come here, you." Without warning, he grabbed Jenny and hugged her. He never thought he'd see the day when he would be so glad to see his sister again. He felt her stiffen in his embrace, but he didn't care. He hugged her anyway. "I love you, Jenny." Wow! Where did that come from? Even *he* hadn't seen *that* one coming. But it wasn't so bad, was it? He thought for a moment, smiling. No, it wasn't bad at all. He really did love his sister, after all. And from now on, he would show it more often, even if *she* didn't appreciate it.

Obviously embarrassed by his sudden attack of affection, Jenny ignored it and acted like it never happened. "And Mrs. Tucker is fit to be tied, too. She thought something must've happened to you and Lisa, so she sent Mr. Tucker to town today to call Mom and Dad at that pest control convention. And poor old Mr. Tucker had to use our rowboat to get to the public landing because you had his speedboat."

She looked past Greg at the stolen speedboat tied to the dock. She wrinkled her nose. "Whose boat is that? Where's Mr. Tucker's boat?"

"It's a long story," Greg said simply. "I'll tell everyone all about it when we go inside." Suddenly a new thought flashed through his mind, and his heartbeat quickened. "Mr. Tucker didn't happen to see Sheriff Clifford in town today, did he?"

"Beats me."

Greg sighed. The feeling of elation from the reunion with his siblings had come to an abrupt end. It was time to worry again. "Where are the Tuckers now?"

"They're inside."

"Then we might as well go in and get this over with," Greg said glumly.

Minutes later, in the Tuckers' living room, Mr. Tucker was livid. "Where have you been!" he demanded, scowling. "We've been worried sick!"

Greg was in no mood for another tongue lashing. He would nip this argument in the bud. Seeing is believing. He removed Rachel's necklace from his pocket. "Do you recognize this, Mr. Tucker?" He dangled the gold heart-shaped charm before the old man's face.

Slowly, Mr. Tucker took the necklace from Greg, turning it over in his gnarled hands, scrutinizing it.

"Let me see that," Mrs. Tucker said, a look of shock and despair on her face.

Mr. Tucker handed it to her. "Where did you get it?" he asked Greg.

"We found it in the trunk of Rachel's car," Greg said softly.

Mrs. Tucker muffled a cry, cupping her hand over her mouth, her eyes filling with tears. She handed the necklace back to Mr. Tucker, then went to the sofa and sat down. "Oh, dear God," she whimpered, dabbing her eyes with a hanky. "Where is she? Where's our Rachel?"

Still clutching the necklace, Mr. Tucker took a seat beside her and stared at the piece of jewelry, turning it over and over in his hands, apparently dazed.

Feeling sorry for them, Greg began relating, as delicately as he could, about discovering Rachel's abandoned and camouflaged car in the woods. He told them all about Whiskers eating the poor fisherman, and how the monster had sunk Mr. Tucker's boat. He told them how he had shot at the beast, hitting it several times, but it hadn't even fazed the monster.

Then he told them how he and Lisa had been arrested and attacked by Sheriff Clifford and that the sheriff had murdered Inspector Gramms in cold blood. When he came to the part about Sheriff Clifford feeding his murder victims to Whiskers, Mr. and Mrs. Tucker both broke down, sobbing in each other's arms.

Greg's heart ached for them. He looked at Jenny, who stood gaping in shock, having heard Greg's incredible story. "Let's give them a moment alone," he said. He ushered Jenny into the kitchen, where Lisa was seated at the table, keeping the twins company.

Earlier, Lisa had suggested she take the twins into the kitchen to have some vanilla ice cream and to keep them out of earshot of Greg's horrific story as he related it to Jenny and the Tuckers.

Greg and Jenny joined them, taking a seat at the kitchen table.

"How'd it go in there?" Lisa asked Greg.

"That was the hardest thing I ever had to do," he said, his elbows resting on the table, cradling his face in his hands.

"I'm sorry *you* had to tell them," Lisa said. "That would've been Inspector Gramms' job. Poor guy."

"Greg ...can you come in here, please?" It was Mr. Tucker calling from the living room, his voice weak and trembling.

Greg hurried into the living room and found Mr. Tucker standing in front of his gun cabinet. The cabinet was open, and Mr. Tucker had removed one of the guns. It was a double-barreled shotgun, and the old man was loading it.

"What are you doing?" Greg asked, puzzled.

"I'm doing what I should've done in the first place," Mr. Tucker replied. "I've known Sheriff Clifford for more than twenty-six years, but I never knew or saw the evil side of him. He's probably got the whole town fooled, and everyone on Mink Lake, too. None of them would ever believe your story, Greg. They're all loyal to Sheriff Clifford—just like I was until you gave me Rachel's necklace. Now I believe you, and I'm sorry I didn't listen to you before."

Having dropped a shell into each of the barrels, Mr. Tucker snapped the gun shut and set it on the floor next to the cabinet. Then he knelt down and began rummaging in the bottom storage compartment of the gun cabinet.

"Mr. Tucker," Greg said, "we have that stolen speedboat. We should all leave here right now—me, you, Mrs. Tucker, Lisa, Jenny, and the twins. We'll take the boat to the public landing, then take your truck south to Woodstream and get help."

"There it is," Mr. Tucker said, apparently ignoring Greg. Then he stood up and turned to Greg. In his hands were a

.38 caliber revolver and a box of bullets. "Load this and keep it in your waistband." He handed the gun and ammo to Greg.

"But I—"

"The south bridge is washed out," Mr. Tucker interrupted. "I heard about it today when I was in town, phoning your parents. Last night's storm washed out the south bridge, so you couldn't get through to Woodstream today, even if you wanted to. The only help is to the north, in Pine Acres. But like you said before, Pine Acres deputies are all pals with Sheriff Clifford. They'd never listen to any of us, wouldn't believe us. And speaking of Sheriff Clifford, I happened to bump into him today when I was in town. I asked him if he had seen you and Lisa. And I had mentioned to him that you were both staying at my place. Of course, that was before I knew he had murdered my granddaughter."

Greg's heart sank. "So sooner or later, he'll probably come looking for us here. And he's probably already disabled *your* truck so we couldn't escape."

"Probably, " Mr. Tucker agreed. "But if he *does* come around here," he nodded at the shotgun and pointed to the .38 in Greg's hand, "at least we'll be ready for him."

"But what about Mom and Dad? You said you called them today?"

"Yes," said Mr. Tucker. "I arranged it so that I would meet them at the public landing tomorrow morning at eight o'clock. At the time, I didn't know where you were with my speedboat, so I was going to use your rowboat and go meet them myself. But now that you have the stolen, er, borrowed, speedboat, we can all go together and meet your parents tomorrow morning at the landing."

"Perfect," said Greg. "Then Dad can take all of us in his station wagon to go get help. But we'll have to drive straight through Pine Acres and go for help in the next town."

"Right," Mr. Tucker agreed. "That would be the town of Axehead—about 50 miles north of Pine Acres."

"What'll we do in the meantime?"

Mr. Tucker grabbed the loaded shotgun, cradled it in his arms. "We stand guard. If that psychopath shows up, at least we'll be fighting him on *our* turf!"

* * *

Later that evening, with the .38 safely tucked into his waistband, Greg asked Lisa to go for a walk with him. They walked hand in hand along the grassy shoreline.

The night was alive with wilderness music. Somewhere across the lake, a lone wolf howled a low, mournful cry. It was quickly answered by a pack of wolves, yipping frantically somewhere far off in the forest. Hundreds of bullfrogs croaked in the darkness surrounding the lake. Their short bursts of chorus sounded like dozens of invisible balloons popping at random in the darkness. Everywhere, the peaceful rhythm of chirping crickets could be heard, their sweet music filling the forest.

A breeze drifted lazily across the lake, and Greg was mesmerized by tiny ripples dancing on the moonlit surface. "Hard to believe something so sinister could be living out there," he said.

"It's a nightmare," Lisa agreed.

Pine boughs whispered in the breeze, and birch leaves fluttered gently. Greg took a deep breath, filling his nostrils with the rich aroma of pine, mixed with the sweet scent of honeysuckle. When he exhaled, he looked at Lisa, who was staring out at the lake. His heart quickened at the sight of her beautiful face aglow in the moonlight. He slipped his arm around her waist, drawing her close. "I can't imagine living my life without you."

She gazed at him, her brown eyes sparkling in the moonlight. "Who says you have to?"

Somewhere on the lake, beyond the shimmering moonlight, a solitary loon unleashed its ghostly wail. Its shrill cry reverberated around the lake and throughout the surrounding forest.

A chilling thought flashed through Greg's mind, shattering the peaceful moment. Somewhere out there in the darkness, perhaps at this very moment, Sheriff Clifford was dumping Inspector Gramms' body into the lake, providing another supper for Whiskers.

CHAPTER 10

The first rays of sunshine burst above the sawtooth horizon, splashing row after row of pine treetops with brilliant hues of orange and yellow. A gray mist hovered above the lake, so thick, Greg could not see more than fifty feet in front of him.

He was standing inside the stolen speedboat, lining up the five milk jugs in a row, on the floor at the rear of the boat. Tucked inside his waistband was the chrome, snub-nosed .38 revolver, fully loaded. He went to the control console, knelt down, and fumbled with the array of wires, searching for the two ignition wires. Lisa's voice behind him startled him.

"Where do you think *you're* going?"

His adrenaline suddenly pumping, he gave her a quick glance, then focused on the wires. "You gave me a scare. What are *you* doing out here?"

She brushed her hair from her eyes. "I heard you get up and go outside. I was worried, wondering what you were up to."

"I couldn't sleep, thinking about that maniac. I lay awake all night, listening for his boat. I thought he might approach Tucker Island any minute."

"And now?"

"Well, I have three hours before we have to meet my mom and dad at the public landing. So I thought I'd do a little hunting." He continued fumbling with the wires beneath the dash. "Which ones are the ignition wires?"

"Greg, why don't you just let the authorities take care of it? That thing is dangerous. Just stay away from it. Please?"

"I already told you, Lisa—this is *my* fight. I can do this. I'll kill that monster once and for all." He looked up at her. "Show me which ones are the ignition wires."

Tears welled in her eyes. "No," she said, shaking her head. "I won't be a part of this. I'm not going to help you get killed. Maybe Mr. Tucker can talk some sense into you." She turned and walked toward the house.

"Lisa! Don't be—"

Suddenly the engine rumbled alive. Obviously the last two wires he touched together were the right ones. He quickly untied the rope and pushed the boat away from the jagged, splintered end of the dock. "Time to go hunting," he told himself. He pushed the throttle all the way forward, and the boat roared, zooming ahead, piercing the clinging haze.

About halfway across the lake, Greg eased up on the throttle, slowing the boat's speed. Then he pulled it all the way back to the upright position, placing it into neutral. The boat came to a stop, lying motionless in the water, the huge motor gurgling softly. Stepping to the rear of the boat, he took a length of rope and tied one end to a milk jug. Then he tied the other end to a cleat on the boat's stern. Using the pair of scissors that he had placed yesterday in the boat's glove compartment, he carefully made one tiny slit at the top of the jug, well above the line of liquid poison. He reasoned that the Chlordane couldn't leak out of the jug until it was squeezed and crushed inside Whisker's mouth.

He lifted the jug, then gingerly lowered it over the side of the boat and into the lake. The lower half of the jug submerged, but the upper half bobbed upright in the calm water.

His plan was to troll with the scented jug, hoping Whiskers would eventually take the bait. But as he was about to push the throttle forward again, distantly he heard the hum of another motor in the dense fog. Then, from the opposite direction, as if it might be coming from the boat landing, he could hear the buzzing sound of yet another motor.

Must be fishermen, he thought. Who else would be out here this early?

He hesitated at the throttle, straining to hear above the boat's gurgling motor, which was still in neutral. Was the sound of the other boat—the first boat he heard—growing louder? Was it getting closer? It was hard to tell over the sputtering noise that his boat was making. He untwisted the ignition wires, cutting the engine. His boat—the stolen boat—was silent.

The other boat *was* getting closer—much closer. In fact, now Greg could hear men's voices above the humming motor, somewhere in the thick fog.

The voices were getting closer.

The boat was getting closer.

Someone was approaching.

Even with the .38 safely tucked inside his waistband, Greg did not want to chance encountering someone. What if he bumped into Sheriff Clifford or some of the sheriff's deputized cronies? They would be armed, too, and Greg would be outnumbered.

Better get out of here, he thought, fumbling for the ignition wires. His hands were trembling. The thought of Sheriff Clifford coming after him had unnerved him. He touched the two wires together. The motor coughed and sputtered. He had dropped the red wire before he could twist it together with the black one.

The engine died.

"Darn!"

The approaching boat was very close now, the voices loud and clear. Only a thin veil of mist separated the two boats.

As Greg was reaching for the wire, something rammed into the rear of his boat, knocking him forward into the windshield, cracking it.

"What the—"

He touched his forehead with his fingertips—it wasn't bleeding—and turned to look over his shoulder. He caught a glimpse of a mammoth black tail, slipping beneath the surface, directly behind the boat.

Greg scrambled to the stern, looking for the steel cleat, from which the milk jug had been tied. He was scared, and yet glad, to discover the cleat had been wrenched completely from the stern. The last thing he wanted was the beast ripping out the entire side of the boat. Not only was the cleat gone, but so were the rope and the jug. "Yes!" he cried, feeling elated. Apparently Whiskers had just eaten a jug of Chlordane.

But would it be enough? he wondered. I still have plenty of rope, and four more jugs. If he wants more, I'll give him mo—

"That *is* our boat!" a male voice said gruffly, interrupting Greg's thoughts.

Greg looked up, surprised. In all the excitement with Whiskers, he had forgotten about the approaching boat, which had penetrated the enveloping fog and was now gliding alongside him.

It was a speedboat, silver-color with red trim. Inside the boat were two burly men, with thick arms and scowling faces.

The driver was wearing a white T-shirt and a blue baseball cap. The other man, standing in the bow, had a beard and was holding a pump-action shotgun. His wild-eyed face was nearly as red as his shirt.

Greg moved swiftly to the console, his hands searching for the ignition wires, while his eyes stayed glued on the two men.

"Hold it right there, pal!" the man with the shotgun yelled. "Don't move!" He was pointing the shotgun at Greg's face, the barrel only a few feet away.

Greg dropped the wires and raised his hands above his head. "This isn't what it looks like," Greg said. "I can explain everything."

Distantly he could still hear the other boat—the one that sounded as if it were coming from the public landing. It sounded closer now, though still lost in the fog. Should he call out? Perhaps someone on the passing boat, concealed in the fog, might hear him, help him. Or maybe he should go for his own gun—the .38 in his waistband. He stared at the single black hole at the end of the shotgun barrel, and decided against it.

The driver boarded Greg's boat—the stolen boat—while the bearded man continued to hold the shotgun on Greg.

The man looked at the stern where the cleat used to be, examining the torn and splintered wood. "Son-of-a—" He cut himself off when he saw the four jugs all lined up neatly in a row on the floor. Then he looked directly at Greg, his face bloated with rage.

"What do you think you're doing?" he barked. "You stole my boat!"

Greg was terrified, and his stomach somersaulted. "I was only borrowing it," he said, his voice shaking. "I was going to return it. Honest!"

The man's eyes widened at the sight of the .38 tucked inside Greg's waistband. The man whisked the gun from Greg's waist. "This is interesting," he said, holding the gun up so his partner could see it. "What's *this* for?"

Greg's mind was reeling with fear and confusion. He was at a lost for words. How could he possibly begin to explain why he was in *their* boat with four jugs of Chlordane and a .38 revolver? "There's been a murder!" he blurted.

The man's eyes suddenly widened another notch. He looked at the .38 in his hand, then suddenly tossed it into the other boat, as if it were a hot potato. "I just got my prints on it!" he cried, wiping his hand on his trousers.

"Who'd you murder, kid?" asked the man with the shotgun.

"I didn't murder anyone!" Greg cried, fisting his hands at his sides. "It was Sheriff Clifford! He killed a state police officer! He shot the guy in cold blood! And I saw him do it!"

The men looked at each other, grinning.

"Looks like we got ourselves a real wise guy, Frank," the man with the shotgun said.

Frank, the man in the T-shirt, took a step closer, looming over Greg. "You stole my boat, punk. You know what we do with punks who steal from us?" The man made a fist. "We teach 'em a lesson ... that's what we do."

The man's right fist shot toward Greg with lightning speed, intended for Greg's stomach.

Greg's reflexes were slightly quicker than Frank's. All the years Greg had spent at the local YMCA, training in karate, would now pay off.

Having just missed Greg's stomach, Frank's hand sailed into the already cracked windshield, smashing through it, severely cutting his hand.

Greg didn't want to fight, but he wasn't about to take a

beating from Frank, who was irate and unreasonable, taking the law into his own hands. Greg had no choice but to defend himself. Instinctively Greg hit Frank in the back of his neck with a closed fist, hoping to stun him and take the fight out of him. The blow made a sickening sound of flesh smacking flesh.

But Frank was a big man, and he simply shook off the blow. As Frank straightened himself up, Greg could hear the other man shouting.

"Get out of the way, Frank! I'll blow his head off! Move!"

Frank ignored him, and glared at Greg, nostrils flared, face red with rage. "I'll kill you!" he hissed. Then he lunged at Greg, both hands outstretched, reaching for Greg's neck.

Again Greg was too swift for the man. He easily sidestepped him. Then, using both fists, he fired three powerful punches, so fast, so hard, Frank didn't have time to block any of them.

One of the blows slammed into Frank's throat, knocking him backwards with tremendous force. His butt slammed into the top edge of the port side, but his upper body continued to sail backward, carried by the momentum. His good hand was twisted behind his back, pinned between the boat and his own body, completely useless.

His shattered hand, torn and bleeding, clawed helplessly at the boat's port side, blood dripping down and smearing across the vinyl interior. With an expression of shear panic, Frank fell backwards between the two boats, splashing headfirst into the lake.

The attack was instantaneous, almost as though the monster had been waiting there all along—waiting for a human morsel. Whisker's cavernous mouth shot straight up out of the water, seized the flailing man, then submerged. The beast was swift and fluid, leaving no trace of its attack.

Horrified, the bearded man screamed, then fired his shotgun, pumping and firing it three times in a frenzy. All three shots blasted harmlessly into the water.

Before the man could pump and fire a fourth time, Whiskers reappeared just beneath the surface and rammed the man's boat. The force of the blow was so great, the boat spun halfway around in the water, so it was now facing the opposite direction.

"Oh, my God!" the man screamed, his face etched in utter terror. Throwing down his gun, he turned the ignition key, starting the engine. Then he thrust the throttle forward and zoomed away, disappearing into the swirling fog.

"WAIT!" Greg yelled, his heart hammering in his chest. He grasped the ignition wires and twisted them together, starting the engine. The boat roared to life, and he wasted no time in getting out of there.

He drove like a dog gone mad, ripping across the lake, trying to catch up with the other boat. Greg thought he might have an ally in the man who had just fired three rounds from his shotgun at Whiskers. Until now, no other adult, besides himself, Lisa, and Sheriff Clifford, had ever seen Whiskers before—and live to tell about it. That man could corroborate parts of Greg and Lisa's story when they went to the authorities—the *real* authorities—for help today. But telling Sheriff Clifford about it would be a deadly mistake for this man.

Watching the man head straight for the public landing, Greg could only assume that he would dock his boat, then drive to town and report this incident to Sheriff Clifford. Adrenaline coursed through every vein in Greg's body as he thought of what might happen to this poor guy if he went to the maniac sheriff and told him he saw Whiskers. If that psychopath will kill a state police officer, Greg thought, he'll kill *anybody!*

Sure enough, a few minutes later, the man reached the landing and quickly docked his boat. As Greg approached the dock in the stolen boat, the man was sprinting through the parking lot and toward a navy blue van.

Having no time to dock his own boat and give chase, Greg shouted to the man to stop.

But it was too late. Greg watched helplessly as the man scrambled into the van and drove off, peeling rubber as he tore out of the parking lot.

"That's just great," Greg said to himself, feeling defeated. "That poor guy will never make it out alive if he goes to Sheriff Clifford."

Having lost the battle, Greg began turning the boat away from the landing, then stopped when something caught his eye. Parked at the far end of the public landing parking lot was Dad's station wagon. Parked next to the wagon was Sheriff Clifford's patrol car. Hitched to the rear of the patrol car was a boat trailer—but no boat.

That must've been the boat he had heard earlier, the one that sounded as if it were coming from the landing.

His mind reeled in horror. If he wasn't unglued enough before, this certainly would push him over the edge. Fear gripped him in its steel jaws, crushing him, smothering him, as the implications of the situation became clear.

Sheriff Clifford has a boat.

Mom and Dad are with him.

They've gone to Tucker Island.

CHAPTER 11

His heart pounding frantically, Greg raced to Tucker Island in the stolen speedboat. All the way there, he kept thinking about Sheriff Clifford and what he was capable of doing.

Please, God, don't let him hurt Mom or Jenny or the twins. Or Lisa. Oh, God ... please don't let him hurt Lisa. What about Dad? He had to think about that one, but only for a second. In spite of all their differences, he couldn't imagine *not* having Dad around as his father.

Please, God, don't let him hurt Dad, either.

Minutes later, he zipped up to the Tuckers' dock, almost crashing into it. He immediately noticed another speedboat tied to one of the thick wooden posts that jutted from the water and projected above the deck. He cut the engine on his boat and glided to a stop alongside the pier and behind the other boat—presumably Sheriff Clifford's boat. With trembling hands, he secured his own boat, then hurried along the dock toward the Tuckers' house.

Suddenly a shot rang out from inside the house.

Greg was already halfway to the house when he heard the blast. He stopped abruptly, blood surging in his ears, his heart banging furiously. Puzzled, he paused to grasp the situation, waiting to see what would happen next. Was *he* being shot at? What should he do? Take cover and just sit there? But what if it wasn't *him* who was being shot at? And if not him, then who? His mind raced, trying to think of what to do next.

Another commotion from inside the house startled him.

There was screaming.

Bloodcurdling screaming.

It was all of them, screaming.

Mom, Jenny, the twins, Lisa—all of them—screaming.

His blood ran cold, and a shiver ran up his spine. He was about to run to the house, when the front door burst open and Jenny sailed out of the house, her eyes bulging with fear. She flew into Greg's arms.

"He shot Dad!" she gasped, her face a ghastly white. Her eyes filled with tears. "He's insane!" Her voice broke and she began to cry. "Oh, God, Greg ...he shot Dad!"

Greg's mind reeled in shocked horror. He didn't know what to do, what to think.

He reached for the .38 in his waistband, then realized the gun was still in the other speedboat, where Frank had tossed it. Images of the crazed sheriff wreaking havoc on his family flashed in his mind. What'll I do? Oh, God! What'll I do? Then something suddenly snapped in his mind.

"This is insane!" he blurted, clenching his fists. "I've got to save them!" He started for the house. "Stay here," he told Jenny. Then—shocked—he stopped abruptly.

Standing in the doorway, her face etched in utter terror, was Lisa. Sheriff Clifford was standing behind her, one hand holding onto her ponytail, the other holding a hunting knife across her throat.

Instinctively Greg called over his shoulder to his sister. "Jenny! Get in the rowboat! Take it and get out of here!

Quick!" Greg knew Jenny had no idea how to drive a speed-boat, so the rowboat, which was docked on the opposite side of the pier as the two speedboats, was the only option. Now that the mad sheriff was obviously bringing the fight to them, Greg wanted her out of harm's way as quickly as possible.

But at the same time, he did not want to take his eyes off of Sheriff Clifford. One of the things he had learned at karate practice was never to take your eyes off your opponent. Always watch your opponent's eyes—that's what his instructor had taught him, for the eyes are like windows to one's soul. By watching the eyes, you were in control, able to read your opponent's mind, ready to react with lightning speed. And being ready was half the battle.

Without saying a word, Jenny scrambled to the rowboat, took a seat, and was reaching for the oars when Sheriff Clifford hollered at her.

"One more move, and I'll cut this one's throat!" Sheriff Clifford shoved Lisa forward, out of the doorway, his massive frame towering over her. "Get out of that boat, sweetheart," he ordered Jenny. He still had the knife at Lisa's throat, and he still clutched her ponytail, using it like a leash.

"Stay where you are, Jenny!" Greg called over his shoulder, never taking his eyes off the sheriff. Then, to Sheriff Clifford he said, "You're a big man ...why don't you come over here and *make* her get out?"

"Greg!" Lisa cried, her eyes filling with tears. "What are you doing!"

Behind him, Greg was aware that Jenny had frozen and remained in the boat.

Sheriff Clifford sneered at Greg, his lips flared, revealing his broken yellow teeth. "Oh, so you wanna play, huh?" He moved forward, pushing Lisa ahead toward the dock, still holding the knife only inches from her throat. "Sure—we can play games," he said, grinning. He had an evil look on his face, resembling a demon from hell. "I *like* playing games. Ya know why? Because I always win! Heh, heh, heh!" He continued moving forward with Lisa.

"Greg—" Lisa whimpered, her voice cracking, tears rolling down her cheeks.

At first Greg was sickened at the ghastly sight before him—sickened and terrified—but then his blood began to boil, and his temper flared. Who did this guy think he was, threatening Greg's family and Lisa this way? Oh, this guy was dangerous, all right. But did he really expect Greg to just stand there and do nothing while his loved ones were being threatened?

Greg had other ideas. Soon his fear melted into a mounting rage—a red-hot rage. His eyes narrowed, and his muscles tightened and bulged, like thick, tough whipcord. "Let her go," he demanded through gritted teeth.

Sheriff Clifford taunted him. "But I thought you wanted to play games."

"Games!" Greg cried. "I don't wanna play games! I wanna *fight!* I know how tough you are with the girls, but how tough are you when it comes to fighting a *man?*"

The remark caused a flicker in the sheriff's eyes—just enough to let Greg know he was beginning to get to the maniac. Keep watching his eyes, he reminded himself. Wait ... and watch.

"How 'bout I kill you first, big man?" the sheriff sneered. "Would you like that?" Greg heard Jenny gasp behind him. Without taking his eyes off the creep, he held his hand, steadying her.

"You talk mighty big for a piece of trash." Adrenaline surged in his veins and blood pounded in his ears. Even though his heart was banging in his chest, he was fearless—absolutely fearless. His brain was now in attack mode, forming a plan. "But what's with all the talk?" Greg went on. He held up his fist. "Why don't you just come over here and get some of this? You're not afraid of me—are you, Sheriff?"

The madman's eyes widened, as he continued walking forward, guiding Lisa ahead of him. They were on the dock now, and getting closer. "Oh, yeah," he sneered. "I'm scared to death of you. Heh, heh, heh."

Greg realized Sheriff Clifford was much bigger than he was, and the sheriff was armed not only with the hunting knife, but with a .357 magnum as well, which hung from a brown leather holster at the madman's side.

Nevertheless, Greg knew, with dead certainty, that he would somehow overpower this raging psychopath. He was baiting him, bit by bit, luring him closer. But his timing would have to be absolutely perfect. He would probably get only one chance to defeat the sheriff. Meanwhile, he would continue waiting, and watching—watching those evil, maniacal eyes.

"Of course you're scared," Greg taunted him. "Only a coward would hold a girl at knifepoint, using her as a shield."

That one got him. Sheriff Clifford suddenly squealed like an animal, dropping his knife hand from Lisa's throat and pushing her aside, causing her to fall into Sheriff Clifford's speedboat, unharmed. He lunged at Greg, the knife still clenched in his hand.

Greg intercepted the hulking sheriff with a powerful kick to his abdomen.

Sheriff Clifford's reflexes were surprisingly quick for a huge man. He jerked his knife hand up just in time to block the kick. In the process, his hand twisted back toward his stomach, and the knife blade slashed across his own stomach. Howling in pain, he dropped the knife and clutched the jagged wound, blood oozing between his fingers, splattering on the dock planks.

Some of the drops of blood fell between the planks and into the lake below.

Seeing the damage he had done with his first blow, Greg moved swiftly with a follow-up kick.

Incredibly, Sheriff Clifford snatched Greg's foot in mid-air, wrenching it back and twisting it with tremendous strength. "You think you can hit me *twice?*" he said, scowling, his eyes bulging, his face insanely distorted. "I don't think so, kid!" He flung the foot aside, flipping Greg into the lake.

Greg hit the water on his belly, his face slapping the surface. Searing pain exploded in his foot, jabbing upward to his knee. Dear, God, don't let it be broken. Not now! As he rolled over in the water, face up, he could hear Jenny screaming.

"Greeeeeeg! Get out of the water!"

He lifted his head, struggled to right himself. He was standing in chest-deep water. He saw Jenny leaning over in the rowboat, pointing to the water behind him.

"Oh, God! It's coming, Greg!" she screamed. "It's coming right at you!"

Greg turned and looked. What he saw terrorized him, making every cell in his body pulse with fear.

A dorsal fin jutted up out of the water, and a pair, of black, ten-foot-long, fleshy whiskers floated on the surface, not more than thirty feet behind him. Whiskers was gliding toward him, stalking him.

He could hear Sheriff Clifford standing on the dock, laughing at him—the psychopath was actually *laughing* at him. The monster was closing—about to have him for supper—and Sheriff Clifford was laughing about it, taunting him.

"Looks like you could use a hand, kid!" he bellowed, holding one hand over his stomach wound. The jagged slash was bleeding profusely. "Heh, heh, heh!"

Greg lunged at the dock, wrapping his arms around a wooden post. He was going to pull himself up onto the dock, but stopped abruptly when he saw Sheriff Clifford draw his .357 magnum from his holster and point it skyward.

Whiskers was gliding silently, steadily towards Greg, just a few feet away.

Greg didn't know which monster to keep his eye on—the insane sheriff, or the giant catfish. He looked from one to the other. Which was the lesser evil of the two? Would he rather be eaten alive, or shot point blank in the face?

Still clutching his stomach with one hand, Sheriff Clifford lowered his weapon and aimed it at the water beyond Greg. "Maybe—just maybe—I'm a good enough shot to kill ole Whiskers before he gobbles you up, eh, kid?" He sighted along the barrel, taking a long, deliberate aim. Then he pulled the trigger.

BOOM!

The bullet ripped into the wooden post, just inches from Greg's face.

"Awww ...now ain't that too bad," the sheriff said mockingly. "I guess I can't aim good with this stab wound and all. Heh, heh, heh! Too bad you cut me, kid. Aww, well ...bon appetite! Heh, heh, heh!"

Whiskers was only two yards away now.

There wasn't time to crawl up on the dock. The monster would be on Greg in a second.

At the last possible moment, his heart thundering, Greg ducked his head under the dock and darted behind the wooden post.

WHAM!

Greg could feel the monster slam into the post on the other side. He watched in terror, as the behemoth shook its colossal head beneath the surface in an apparent act of fury. Greg felt one of its tendrils slap against his ankle beneath the water. The shear power behind that single whisker was frighteningly awesome.

With one flick of its enormous tail, Whiskers shot away from the dock, disappearing into deeper water.

There was no time to lose. Greg realized this was his only chance to get out of there before the monster returned to finish the job.

He bobbed out from under the dock, pushed off the sandy bottom with his good foot, and threw himself halfway across the dock, scraping his chin and stomach on the rough-hewn planks. He was about to swing his legs out of the water, when Sheriff Clifford stood above him, his boots planted firmly in front of Greg's face.

"Where ya think you're going?" the sheriff asked, prodding Greg's head with a heavy boot. His voice was laced with menace.

Greg glanced up and was horrified to see that the madman had the .357 magnum pointed down at Greg's head. Now what? What could he possibly do to get out of *this* one? Think, kid! Think!

Sheriff Clifford cocked the revolver.

The hammer locked back to the firing position with a loud ... CLICK! "You can't leave yet, son. Ole Whiskers hasn't had his breakfast yet. Heh, heh, heh!"

The maniac began stepping on Greg's head, mashing the side of Greg's face into the planks. Blood dripped from the sheriff's wound, splattering on Greg's face and the surrounding boards—and between the boards and into the lake below.

Before Greg could react, a gunshot exploded above him.

BOOM!

A bullet ripped through the planking, just inches from his nose.

Then another shot.

BOOM!

This one tore through the wood, next to the first one, and wood splinters erupted around Greg's face.

Another shot. BOOM!

Then another. BOOM!

Greg tried to raise himself from the deck, but the towering sheriff was too heavy, too strong. This was torture—sheer torture.

He didn't want to die this way—at the hands of a psychopathic killer—the madman who shot Dad—oh, God, poor Dad—please don't let him be dead. Please don't let this maniac hurt the others. Oh, God! Please!

"This last bullet's got your name on it, kid," Sheriff Clifford sneered, pressing down harder on Greg's head.

The pressure was tremendous, the pain unbearable. Death by Whiskers would be better than this—a hundred times better, he thought. If I could only get my hands on that psycho—

"Get off of him!" Greg heard Lisa scream, and suddenly the pressure on his head was gone. He was able to squeeze his head out from under the sheriff's boot. He looked up just in time to see Sheriff Clifford backhand Lisa across her face, sending her sprawling on the deck. Apparently she had rushed up behind him and pushed, causing him to stumble and lose his balance, just enough to relieve the pressure from Greg's head.

Now the sheriff, still clutching the .357, was glaring at Lisa. "That will cost you, sweetheart," he said grinning. He pointed the gun down at her, and she threw her hands up, blocking her face defensively.

It was now or never. Greg had only a millisecond to react before the madman could pull the trigger. He threw his arms around the big man's ankles and pulled up with all his might, simultaneously pushing his shoulder into the Sheriff's shins.

Sheriff Clifford stumbled backward, momentarily, trying to aim his gun at Greg while fighting to keep his balance.

Greg mustered a new surge of energy, shoving and lifting as hard as he could, straining muscles in his back and arms that he never knew he had before. The sheriff teetered at the edge of the dock, blood spewing from his stomach, staining his tan shirt bright red. His gun hand wavered as he tried to aim the weapon at Greg's head.

Greg heaved against the sheriff's legs with yet another burst of energy, a final thrust of power.

"Aaah!" the sheriff cried, falling into the lake.

SPLASH!

The big man poked his head above the surface, followed by his hand, still clutching the gun. His eyes locked on Greg's, who was now standing safely on the dock.

The sheriff aimed his gun directly at Greg. "So long, son. Too bad ... you almost made it. Heh, heh, heh!" He began squeezing the trigger.

Suddenly Sheriff Clifford jerked forward, as though he had lost his footing, and the gun fired at that instant—BOOM!—shooting harmlessly into the water. The sheriff had a strange look on his face—a look of surprise and disbelief. Then his eyes widened—bulged—to the point that Greg thought they would pop from their sockets. Suddenly the sheriff's look of disbelief turned into one of utter horror.

At that moment, Greg saw it—the black dorsal fin and the black fleshy tendrils stretched across the water directly behind the madman.

Whiskers!

Sheriff Clifford spun around in the water, facing the behemoth. "Get away from me!" he boomed, slapping the water in front of him.

Whisker's massive head surfaced only a few feet from Sheriff Clifford, its black beady eyes staring at him, locking in on him. The monster glided closer, within arms reach.

"Get away from me!" Sheriff Clifford shouted, slamming his fist into the giant's head. "You can't eat me, you dumb beast! I took care of you, fed you. You need me!"

The monster opened its cavernous mouth and, in one fluid motion, inhaled the sheriff, pinning him between its colossal jaws.

Sheriff Clifford unleashed a bone-chilling scream—a scream so loud that Greg was certain it could be heard clear around the lake. Dangling from the monster's massive mouth, the sheriff clawed and pounded at the smooth black snout, but to no avail.

With a sudden thrust of its powerful tail, Whiskers submerged with the sheriff, his arms and legs still thrashing frantically.

Then ... silence.

CHAPTER 12

Greg stood on the dock, hugging Lisa and Jenny, who were both crying tears of relief.

"Is he dead?" Jenny asked, sobbing. "Is that maniac really gone?"

"Yes, Jenny," Greg said, stroking her hair. "Sheriff Clifford is gone."

"Thank God!" Lisa cried, dabbing her eyes with the back of her hand.

"Yes," Greg agreed. "Thank God." He herded them toward the house. "Come on ... let's go check on Dad."

Inside the Tuckers' house, Greg found Mom, the twins, and the Tuckers all gathered around Dad, who was lying on the kitchen floor with a bullet hole in his shoulder.

His shoulder! Thank God it was only his shoulder! Mrs. Tucker, who was kneeling next to Dad, dressing the wound, assured Greg that Dad would be okay *if* he received medical attention without delay.

Greg felt immense relief. After explaining to everyone what had just happened to Sheriff Clifford, he went to Mom, who was crying, and put his arms around her, reassuring her. "It's okay, Mom. Don't cry."

"Oh, Greg," she sobbed, "if anything happened to you or your father, I wouldn't know what I'd do!"

"It's okay, Mom. We're all okay, and Dad is gonna be all right, too." Greg glanced at the twins, who were completely engrossed in Mrs. Tucker's expert bandaging job.

"After we spoke to Mr. Tucker yesterday," Mom went on, "we were so worried about you and Jenny and the twins, we couldn't sleep. So we got up and started back to Mink Lake earlier than we had planned."

"Is Daddy gonna die?" Timmy suddenly chimed in, looking up with his freckled, tearstained face.

"I hope not!" Tommy blurted, his eyes still red with tears. "I love my Daddy!"

"Me, too!" Timmy cried.

Sniffling, Jenny kneeled and swooped the twins in her arms, kissing each boy on his head.

Greg smiled. "Don't worry, guys. Dad is going to be all right. I promise." He looked at Dad, smiling, but was shocked to see that Dad wasn't smiling back.

Instead of smiling, Dad was scowling at him. "You think you're in a position to be making any promises?" he snapped. He grimaced in pain when he tried to raise himself on his elbows.

"Now take it easy, Sam," Mrs. Tucker scolded. "Or you'll get the bleeding to start all over again."

Dabbing her tears, Mom turned to Dad and said, "Sam, please don't start anything now." Her voice quivered, and she looked at Greg, her lips trembling.

"When we got back to town this morning," Mom explained, "we were too early to meet you guys at the public landing as planned, and there was no way to reach you by phone. So we went straight to Sheriff Clifford's office and told him about Mr. Tucker's phone call yesterday. We asked him if he had any idea of what was going on out here, but the sheriff said everything was fine, that Mr. Tucker was getting old and senile and that we should just ignore him. Then he *insisted* on taking your father and me to Tucker Island in *his* boat."

"Old and senile!" Mr. Tucker cried indignantly. "Hmmpf! I should have shot him when I seen him coming up the walk!"

Greg was wondering what had happened to their plan. Mr. Tucker was supposed to be standing guard with his shotgun, just in case Sheriff Clifford showed up—which he had. "Why *didn't* you shoot him?" Greg asked.

Mom jumped in before the old man could answer. "Mr. Tucker warned Sheriff Clifford not to come any closer, but he just waved Mr. Tucker off, telling him that he was with us, and that everything was okay. But when we got inside, Sheriff Clifford drew his gun and forced all of us into the basement. But just before he slammed the basement door and locked us in, he grabbed poor Jenny."

Jenny stood up from the twins and went to Mom, embracing her. Then Mom continued.

"He only had her for a second, and she was screaming the whole time—just screaming! Your father broke the door in and tried to overpower the sheriff."

"And that's when your Dad got shot and Jenny ran out of the house," Lisa added. "He shot him right here in the kitchen."

"Holy cow!" Greg said incredulously. He looked at Dad, who was sitting up, leaning against the kitchen cabinets. "You could've been killed, Dad."

"That's right, Greg!" Dad snapped. "You could've gotten us all killed!"

"Now, Sam," Mom said sternly. "Don't start!"

Dad ignored her, fueling his own anger. "You should've gone for help a long time ago—before everything got out of hand. Can't you do anything right? You should've taken better care of your sister and brothers. I just assumed you were man enough to do at least *that* much. But I guess I was wrong!"

Greg gaped at Dad in shocked disbelief, his mouth hanging open. He was completely speechless. This was incredible! Was Dad blaming *him* for Whiskers and Sheriff Clifford? What in the world is going on here? *He* didn't do anything wrong. Couldn't Dad see that? Didn't Dad realize *he* had just saved everybody's life? Including Dad's? If he hadn't defeated Sheriff Clifford, they could *all* be dead right now. Sheriff Clifford was gone, thanks to *him*.

Suddenly Greg's feeling of immense relief for Dad was boiling away—boiling into an intense hatred for Dad, instead. He bit his lip, frowning. Maybe a shoulder wound wasn't enough for Dad. Maybe Sheriff Clifford should've aimed a little higher.

A pang of guilt ripped through Greg, but the thought remained, nevertheless.

Mrs. Tucker broke the dead silence by coaxing Dad to get up carefully from the kitchen floor. "You have to go to the hospital in Pine Acres, Sam, as soon as possible. The bullet is still lodged in your shoulder." She wiped her hands on her apron. "It's going to need some work."

"I'll take him," Mr. Tucker volunteered.

"Oh, no you won't!" Mrs. Tucker scolded. "You'll stay right here and help me watch over the little ones. You've had enough excitement for one day, old man." She cupped her hands protectively around Timmy and Tommy's heads. "Besides, Sam is going to need a strong shoulder to lean on. I think Greg should take him."

"So do I," Jenny chimed in.

"Yeah, I'll take him," Greg said, his anger still smolder-

ing. He stood behind Dad, hooked his hands into Dad's arm-
pits, and helped him up. "Let's go, Dad."

"I'll go with," Mom offered.

"Me too," Lisa said.

"No!" Greg said firmly. "Whiskers is still out there somewhere. I don't want you two to go along. It's not safe."

He draped Dad's arm around his own shoulders, steadying him. "You guys wait here until the state police have a
chance to come out and kill that monster. I'll phone them
from the hospital."

"Hey, Greg!" Dad said curtly.

"What?"

"Just forget about this Whiskers nonsense and get me to
the hospital. You think you can handle *that* much?"

Greg rolled his eyes, fuming inside. He looked at Mom
and Lisa. "We're going now, and you're staying here. Wait for
the state police."

Lisa tiptoed in front of Greg and kissed him on the mouth.
"Be careful." She looked around the room at the others, who
were watching her. Ignoring her audience she said, "I love
you, Greg."

It was almost enough to make Greg forget about his seeth-
ing anger for Dad. Almost.

"I love you, too."

Later, at the Tuckers' dock, Greg helped Dad into the
stolen speedboat.

"What are those?" Dad asked, pointing to the four jugs
of Chlordane.

Greg knew Dad would explode when he explained what
he was doing with Dad's Chlordane. But right now, Greg didn't
really care because he was so angry himself. Besides, what
difference would it make if Dad got mad at him? Dad was
always getting mad him anyhow.

He told Dad what was in the jugs and what he was using them for.

As predicted, Dad exploded.

"What the hell is wrong with you!" he barked. "That Chlordane will kill everything in the lake! Are you sitting on your brains? If the Department of Natural Resources caught you with that stuff in unlabeled jugs, in a boat—a *stolen* boat, at that—going across the lake, they'd fine you and throw you in jail!"

He was furious, his face as red as the blood seeping through his bandage. "Get that stuff off this boat! NOW!" Using his good arm, he grabbed one of the jugs and thrust it at Greg. "Take it!" he commanded.

Enraged, Greg ignored him. He went to the console and hot-wired the engine, starting the boat. Then he untied the mooring rope and shoved off from the dock.

The boat was still in neutral, unmoving.

Dad loomed over him, still clutching the jug of Chlordane in his good hand. He jammed his face into Greg's face. "Turn it off, or I'll break you in half—bullet wound or no bullet wound!" he shouted.

That did it! Something inside of Greg just snapped. "SIT DOWN AND SHUT UP!" he yelled, glaring at Dad. Then he jammed the throttle all the way open, and the boat lurched forward with a sudden, powerful jolt.

Dad stumbled backwards and fell over the starboard side— into the lake—taking the jug of Chlordane with him.

The boat had already zoomed several feet ahead, before Greg realized Dad had fallen overboard.

"Oh, my God!" Greg cried.

He jerked the throttle back, slowing the boat immediately. He was going to put the boat into reverse, then realized it would be quicker to just turn the boat around, instead. He shoved the throttle forward and cranked the steering wheel hard left.

The motor died.

His heart thundering, Greg frantically checked the red and black ignition wires.

The wires were still twisted together, as they should be.

What was wrong? What could it be? What? Think! Think!

In a panic, now Greg wished with all his heart that he had brought Lisa along. She's a mechanic. And a darn good one!

But Lisa's not here. No—thanks to him, Lisa's back in the house, where he had ordered her to stay.

That was stupid!

The engine must be flooded. That's it! Must've flooded it from throwing it into forward, then jerking it back into neutral, then forward again.

Darn it!

He glanced at Dad, who was just now getting on his feet, standing almost up to his neck in water. He was holding his wounded shoulder, squinting in pain. The entire bandage was now stained red with blood.

The jug of Chlordane floated freely in front of him.

Greg knew Dad was in grave danger. But what could he do? The boat was thirty or forty feet away from Dad. Greg called out to him, keeping his eye on the surrounding water. "Dad! Grab the jug of—"

Whiskers popped up from beneath the surface, just three feet in front of Dad, inhaled the jug, then submerged in a single, arched movement, its sleek black skin glistening in the sunlight.

Greg had always known Dad to be a tough, no-nonsense kind of guy, never scared or worried about anything, always in control. The fact that Dad had kicked in the basement door to rescue Jenny from Sheriff Clifford—*that* was Dad. So when Greg saw the look of indescribable terror on Dad's face, he barely recognized him. It didn't even *look* like Dad.

"GREG!" Dad screamed, his face pasty white. He tried swimming toward the boat, but his shoulder gave out immediately. He stood, clutching his shoulder, wincing with pain. "GREEEEEG!"

Greg's heart thumped in his chest, his guts churning, somersaulting, a million butterflies fluttering all at once inside his stomach. Adrenaline pumped through his system, and he fought hard to control his panic. His mind reeled in a horrific kaleidoscope of frantic thoughts.

Got to save him. Can't let him die. I can't! Whiskers! Whiskers will get him! Eat him! Whiskers is going to eat Dad! Do something! Now! Do it now! What? Do what? Anything! Think, man! Think! Do *something!*

Greg eyed the remaining three jugs of Chlordane on the floor at the rear of the boat. He snatched one up and scrambled to the boat's glove box to retrieve the scissors he had left there. Then he pierced the jug above the fill line and held it up, getting ready to toss it underhand into the water.

He eyed the water surrounding Dad. "DAD!" he yelled. "MOVE BACK TOWARD THE DOCK. GET OUT OF THE WATER!"

But Dad was terrified, frozen in place. He didn't move, *couldn't* move.

This wasn't the Dad that Greg knew. He had never seen Dad like this before—petrified and completely helpless. Dad *needed* Greg's help. His life *depended* on Greg's help.

Greg knew, all too well, that Dad would perish in a matter of seconds, if he didn't do something—NOW! RIGHT NOW!

Greg lobbed the jug into the lake, and it landed about ten feet away from Dad.

SPLASH! The jug floated upright, but almost completely submerged.

Dad jerked his head in the direction of the splash, his eyes bulging from their sockets, reflecting the unmistakable look of panic—sheer panic—on his face.

"GO TO THE DOCK!" Greg screamed. "GET OUT OF THE WATER!"

Dazed and gasping for air, Dad stared in shock all around him. Clearly he was having a panic attack. This big, tough man, whom Greg had known all his life—a symbol of strength and character, a rugged, rock-solid individual to whom you could turn to in time of need for support or protection, a man who had the guts to go after Sheriff Clifford, risking his own life to save his daughter—was having a panic attack!

Greg had never known that Dad was prone to panic attacks, and if he hadn't seen him with his own eyes—standing in the water, bleeding from his shoulder, bewildered and terrified, frozen in place—he would have never believed it. Suddenly he felt pity for Dad, standing there so helpless, so weak and vulnerable. Dad was only seconds away from becoming Whisker's next meal, and this time there was nothing Dad could do to save himself.

It's up to me, Greg thought. *I* have to save him. He picked up another jug of Chlordane, carefully pierced its top with the scissors, then tossed it into the lake, away from Dad. His plan, his hope, was to divert the monster's attention off of Dad and onto the jug, maybe giving Dad enough time to get away.

The jug splashed in the water, close to the other one.

Whiskers exploded through the surface, directly beneath the floating jugs, inhaling them. The momentum of its thrust carried it skyward, its upper torso six or seven feet above the water, its sleek black skin glistening in the sun. Then the giant catfish came crashing down, slamming into the surface with a tremendous splash. When it hit the water, it fell momentarily beneath the surface, then bounced back up, its colossal body shuddering. The monster thrashed on the surface, its enormous tail flailing back and forth.

The powerful tail struck Dad in the head, spilling him backwards, knocking him underwater.

Greg watched, horrified, waiting for Dad to resurface.

He didn't.

With a final flick of its huge tail, Whiskers submerged beneath the surface, a small wake trailing after the giant.

Eyeing the last remaining jug of Chlordane at the rear of the boat, Greg snatched it up, pierced it, then stood on the stern and jumped into the lake. There was no time to lose— Dad would drown, if he wasn't eaten first. There was no way to swim to Dad with the jug in hand, but luckily the water was just beneath Greg's chin. Holding the jug above the surface, he forced his way through the water and toward Dad, who was only thirty feet away.

At first, Greg didn't know if it was worth his trouble to carry the jug with him and risk slowing him down. After all, Whiskers had already swallowed four gallons of the poison. Was it having any effect on him at all? But after watching Whiskers struggling to dive, perhaps there was a chance the pesticide was working.

As he approached Dad, floating face down in the water, out of reach of the dock and too far from the boat, he was glad he had brought the Chlordane with him. He clung to the jug as if it were a protective shield. "DAD!" he cried, lifting Dad's head out of the water. His face was blue, his eyes closed.

Greg was about to pinch his nose shut and breathe into his mouth, when Dad's eyes suddenly fluttered open.

"Greg?" he asked weakly.

"It's okay, Dad," Greg said, hooking his arm around Dad's neck, holding Dad's head out of the water. Using the water's buoyancy, he began floating and pulling Dad toward the dock. "Hold on, Dad. I'll have you out of here in a minute." With his free hand, he continued to hold the jug above water.

Too late.

Whiskers surfaced only ten feet away, its black beady eyes staring at Greg.

Apparently Dad saw the monster, too, for he started flailing his arms and legs. "GREEEEG!" he screamed, thrashing the water.

Greg tightened his grip around Dad's neck, keeping his face above water. He's panicking. Got to keep his head out of the water. He doesn't know what he's doing. Got to help him. Save him.

Silently, deliberately, Whiskers glided toward them, its coal-black eyes penetrating Greg, sending a chill up his spine.

The monster stopped abruptly, shuddering on the surface. Its long, fleshy whiskers twitched spasmodically in the water.

Keeping an eye on the giant catfish, Greg continued dragging Dad through water and toward the dock. "Almost there, Dad."

Whiskers resumed its attack, gliding toward them, his staring eyes locked on Greg's.

It's getting too close. Can't move fast enough. It's too big. Too fast!

Now *Greg* was fighting back panic. The monster was almost on top of him, looming in front of him. When the creature opened its cavernous mouth, Greg rammed the jug of Chlordane deep into its throat, almost losing his arm in the process.

"DIE, BEAST! DIE!" he screamed.

The massive jaws sprung shut, narrowly missing Greg's arm. With a single powerful thrust of its tail, Whiskers disappeared beneath the surface.

Silence.

"Come on, Dad," Greg said, pulling him through the water. "We're almost there."

The dock was only a few yards away now. Just a few short yards to safety. Whiskers surfaced again, not more than six feet away, working its jaws, shaking its enormous head.

"COME ON!" Greg shrieked at the beast. "That's *five* gallons of Chlordane! What does it take to kill you!"

Its black beady eyes locked on Greg's, and Whiskers moved in for the kill.

Greg braced himself for the attack, his fist raised, ready to strike the beast with everything he had—win, lose, or draw.

Whiskers glided forward. Then, only four feet away from Greg and Dad, the monster suddenly flipped over onto its back, its creamy white belly bobbing on the surface. It thrashed and shuddered, splashing water on Greg and Dad.

It thrashed furiously, apparently trying to right itself. Its huge tail raised almost straight up out of the water, then slammed down on the surface.

SMACK!

The giant did not, *could* not submerge.

Greg watched in shocked disbelief. After swallowing five gallons of poison, the monster was still alive.

"DIE!" he screamed, adrenaline surging in his veins, his heart pounding.

Whiskers' enormous tail slapped the surface again and again, its giant body thrashing and churning. Again it tried to dive, but quickly sprung back to the surface, convulsing.

Then, with a final violent shudder, the monster lay still, its giant white belly bobbing lifeless above the surface.

Whiskers was dead.

EPILOGUE

Greg watched in awe as the Wisconsin Department of Natural Resources' (DNR) helicopter airlifted Whiskers' giant carcass from Mink Lake.

"God, it's *big!*" Lisa cried, standing next to Greg, holding his hand.

Tucker Island was swarming with statepolice, DNR personnel, state biologists, officials from the Environmental Protection Agency (EPA) and the Center for Disease Control (CDC), and TV camera crews and reporters from all over the country.

Mr. Cogburn, an investigator with the DNR, had just completed an interview with Greg, finally giving him the opportunity to tell his story to the authorities. Of course, there were plenty of reporters and cameramen on hand, too, to record every word of Greg's story.

The DNR had rigged a makeshift litter for the giant carcass. The litter was made of steel cables and several yards of tough canvas material.

Greg watched as the helicopter, roaring thirty feet above the water, strained against the tremendous weight of Whiskers' dead body. Its huge head and tail hung limply from either end of the litter. As the helicopter climbed, the steel cables stretched tight, then the canvas sling was pulled taut.

The giant catfish resembled a small black submarine, dangling above the lake.

"AWESOME!" Greg shouted above the roar of the helicopter.

The helicopter pointed toward the public landing, then whisked the giant away.

"Where are they taking him?" Lisa asked, holding her hand above her brow, shielding her eyes from the sun.

"Mr. Cogburn from the DNR said they're gonna take Whiskers to the state university in Madison," Greg said. "That's where they'll do an autopsy on him, and study his tissue samples and stuff."

"So they think Sheriff Clifford may be right about the radiation leaking from the nuclear power plant into the Wolverine River, then into Mink Lake?" Lisa asked.

"Oh, yeah," Greg said matter-of-factly. "Mr. Cogburn says the EPA has already confirmed the leak. And they think the radiation *was* the cause for Whiskers' abnormal size."

"Just like what happened in the Chernobyl nuclear meltdown in the Soviet Union, back in the 80's."

"Right," Greg agreed. "In that instance, there were all kinds of animals born deformed, and fish that grew to humongous size."

"When you say fish, you mean more than one, right?"

"Yeah," Greg said. "In the Chernobyl case, there were *several* fish of abnormal size."

"So there could be more than one Whiskers out there," Lisa said, nodding toward the lake.

"Mr. Cogburn doesn't think so, but he says it *is* possible."

Lisa shivered and crossed her arms. *"That's* a creepy thought."

"Yeah," Greg agreed, slipping his arm around her shoulders. "I wouldn't wish another Whiskers on my worst enemy. Mr. Cogburn says the DNR is going to shock the lake with electricity."

"What for?"

"That's how they survey the lake's fish population," Greg explained. "They shock the water, which stuns the fish, and then the fish float to the surface, where they can count them, or in this case, just observe them."

"So the shocking doesn't harm them?" Lisa asked.

"No. And that way they can tell for sure whether or not there are anymore monsters out there."

"Then the sooner they shock the lake, the better."

"Exactly," Greg said.

He heard Mom calling his name.

"Greg!"

He turned and saw Mom waving at him from the end of the Tuckers' dock. She was standing next to Dad, who was lying on a stretcher, surrounded by paramedics, clad in white uniforms. They were loading Dad into an ambulance boat for the trip to the public landing. From there they would take Dad to the hospital in Pine Acres.

Mom motioned for Greg to come over.

"They're ready to take Dad to the hospital now," Mom said. "But he wants to say good-bye to you first."

Dad wants to say good-bye to *me?* Greg thought, surprised.

Dad was strapped to the gurney, nestled inside the medical emergency boat.

A paramedic—a blond woman, about 30 years-old—was hooking up an I.V. to Dad's wrist.

"How ya doing, Dad?" Greg asked, as he and Lisa approached him.

Dad held up his hand, smiling warmly at Greg. "Hi, son," he said cheerily. "I'm fine ... thanks to you."

Greg took his hand, shaking it, smiling back.

"You saved my life, Greg," Dad said. He looked away abruptly, his lips quivering. Then, his eyes filling with tears, he looked directly at Greg. "You did fine, son. You saved my li—" His voice cracked, and he swallowed hard, fighting back his tears. "I lov—" He shook his head slowly, biting his lip, his voice broken.

Dad's obvious emotion triggered a flood of emotion in Greg, as well.

Suddenly Greg found himself fighting back tears, a lump throbbing in his throat, his eyes burning. He took a deep breath ...exhaled. "I'm glad you're all right, Dad."

Dad stretched his good arm up, reaching out to Greg, tears flowing down his face and onto the pillow.

Greg leaned into the outstretched arm, and Dad pulled him close, hugging him tight.

It was the warmest hug Greg had ever known—the hug that he had been missing for all these years.

Greg hugged him back with earnest. "I love you, Dad," he said, his voice quivering. He could feel Dad's chest heaving beneath him, as Dad sobbed.

"I-I lov—"Dad's voice broke again.

"I know," Greg squeaked, his own voice broken. "I know."

* * *

The next day, Greg was standing outside his cabin, talking with Lisa. Mom had just left for the hospital in Pine Acres to go visit Dad. Greg was in charge of watching over Jenny and the twins. Jenny was inside, lying on the couch, reading a romance novel. The twins were down on the beach, playing in the sand with their plastic pails and shovels.

As Greg chatted with Lisa, he knew it was only a matter

of time before one of the twins would come charging up the hill, tattling on the other twin for destroying his sand castle, or throwing sand in his face, or calling him a name, or any other of a thousand squabbles that only Timmy and Tommy could possibly come up with.

"Vacation's almost over," Lisa said, walking over to the twins' blue and white swing set. She sat down in a canvas swing and began swinging lightly. "You'll be going home soon ... back to Illinois." She pursed her lips, staring down at the ground while she swung. "We probably won't see each other again until next summer." She glanced up at him, then down again, staring at the ground. "It's gonna be a long winter," she said coyly.

Greg sat down in the swing next to her, watching her, pondering. He hadn't thought of what would become of their relationship once his vacation was over. What *would* they do? He wasn't even sure they *had* a relationship, just because they had said they loved one another. *Did* he love her?—this beautiful redhead sitting next to him, so radiant, so lovely, so ...*loving*. That was the key word—loving. Lisa was *loving*. He felt loved by her—a genuine, heartwarming love.

Suddenly Greg realized they most definitely had a relationship. Of course they did. He loved her!—a deep and profound love—and he knew he would never say good-bye to her ...no matter what.

"Of course, I was planning to go back to college this fall, anyway," Lisa continued. "And I was thinking of getting a part-time mechanic job at a garage. Plenty of cars that need repairing." She sighed. "And you'll be starting college soon."

Greg got off his swing, stood before her, and grasped the metal chains that supported her swing, stopping her abruptly.

She looked up, surprised. "What are you—"

He bent over and kissed her.

It was a long, warm, tender kiss.

When it was over, she smiled at him, her eyes flashing.

He cupped her chin in his hand and said, "Wherever we gotta go, whatever we gotta do—we'll still be together. And I'm *not* gonna wait 'til next summer to see you again. No way!"

He leaned forward to kiss her again, but a scream from Tommy stopped him cold.

"GREEEEEEEEEEEG!"

It wasn't the whining wail of a tattletale. This scream was shrill, urgent ...and bloodcurdling. It was the kind of scream that immediately filled Greg with ice-cold, gut-wrenching dread.

Greg spun on his heels, almost knocking Lisa out of her swing. As he raced down the hill, he was barely aware of Jenny dashing out the cabin door behind him.

"Oh, God, Greg!" she gasped. "Not again!"

Tommy was already near the top of the hill, panting, his face ghastly white. "Catfish got Timmy!" he sputtered, his eyes wide with alarm. He was pointing toward the beach. "Catfish got Tim—"

Greg was gone, flying down the hill past Tommy, his heart in his throat. When he reached the beach, his dread immediately turned to confusion.

Timmy was standing only a foot from the shoreline, in six inches of water, crying hysterically. His left hand was completely wrapped around his right index finger, cradling it.

"Timmy, what's wrong?" Greg asked, studying him, his eyes searching for bite marks or open wounds on the boy.

There were none.

Jenny, Lisa, and Tommy rushed up behind Greg, the three of them out of breath.

"What is it, Timmy?" Jenny asked, puffing. "What's wrong?"

Crying uncontrollably, Timmy let go of his finger long enough to point at his feet. "The catfish got me, Gweg," he sobbed, his freckled face glistening beneath his tears.

"What catfish?" Greg asked, confused, looking down at the shallow water. Then he saw them—a school of tiny, black catfish minnows, swarming around Timmy's feet, darting here and there between his ankles.

"They're only minnows," Greg said, relieved. "They can't hurt you unless—Timmy, you didn't try to pick one up, did you?"

"Yeah," Tommy volunteered. "Me and Timmy was twying to catch one, and it bit him."

"No, no, no, you guys," Greg scolded softly, studying the wounded finger. "You can't pick them up. They have a stinger in their fins, like a bee. If you touch one, you'll get stung and it'll feel just like a bee sting."

"Ouch!" Lisa said, grimacing. "That's gotta hurt!"

Tommy jabbed his hands on his hips. *"Now* you tell us!" he said, rolling his eyes. "Tewwific!"

Everyone laughed, except Timmy. He was clutching his finger again. "Will it be all wight, Gweg?" he asked, sniffling.

"Yes, Timmy," Greg said, putting his hand on Timmy's freckled shoulder.

"Come on—let's go put something on it to make it feel better."

"All wight. Then I can have some ice cweam ...wight, Gweg?"

"Me, too!" Tommy chimed in. "I want ice cweam, too!"

"Okay, okay," Greg said, chuckling. "I'll get the iodine and a BAND-AID, and Jenny can get the ice cream."

"Yea!" Tommy cheered. "Ice cweam!" He turned to Timmy and said, "I'll wace ya! Last one there's a wotten egg!" Then he turned and raced up the hill.

Timmy suddenly forgot his injury and dashed up the hill after Tommy. "No fair, Tommy!" he cried. "You started be-ffffor me!"

Shaking their heads, laughing, Jenny and Lisa started up the hill after the twins.

Greg turned to follow them, then stopped abruptly. Something out of the corner of his eye had attracted his attention. But what? What was it? He faced the lake, gazing out at the vast body of water.

The lake shimmered under a glaring sun.

A pair of white sea gulls flitted above the water, apparently in search of a fish lunch.

Off in the distance, a loon bobbed in the water. Its sleek black head, jutting from the surface, resembled a small periscope.

Greg thought he had glimpsed something else in the water—something long, black, and slender. Like a floating tendril. Or a whisker!

"No way," Greg said, shaking his head. "Definitely not."

As he started up the hill, his back to the lake, the loon shrieked its ghostly laughter behind him.

www.ingramcontent.com/pod-product-compliance
Lightning Source LLC
Chambersburg PA
CBHW020613120726
47905CB00003B/781